DEEP IN THE WILD: MAMMOTH
BY
GERRY GRIFFITHS

SEVERED**PRESS**

DEEP IN THE WILD: MAMMOTH

Copyright © GERRY GRIFFITHS

WWW.SEVEREDPRESS.COM

ISBN: 978-1-922861-82-5

ALSO BY GERRY GRIFFITHS

DEATH CRAWLERS SERIES
DEATH CRAWLERS (BOOK 1)
DEEP IN THE JUNGLE (BOOK 2)
THE NEXT WORLD (BOOK 3)
BATTLEGROUND EARTH (BOOK 4)
CRYPTID ZOO SERIES
CRYPTID ZOO (BOOK 1)
CRYPTID COUNTRY (BOOK 2)
CRYPTID ISLAND (BOOK 3)
CRYPTID CIRCUS (BOOK 4)
CRYPTID NATION (BOOK 5)
CRYPTID KINGDOM (BOOK 6)
CRYPTID FRONTIER (BOOK 7)
DEEP IN THE WILD SERIES
DEEP IN THE WILD: SABERTOOTH (BOOK 1)
DEEP IN THE WILD: DIRE WOLVES (BOOK 2)
DEEP IN THE WILD: HELL PIGS (BOOK 3)
DEEP IN THE WILD: TRIBESMEN (BOOK 4)
DEEP IN THE WILD: SURVIVAL (BOOK 5)
DEEP IN THE WILD: MONGRELS (BOOK 6)
STAND-ALONE NOVELS
SILURID
THE BEASTS OF STONECLAD MOUNTAIN
DOWN FROM BEAST MOUNTAIN
TERROR MOUNTAIN

DEEP IN THE WILD: MAMMOTH
(DEEP IN THE WILD: BOOK 7)

DEDICATION

To those that open their hearts
to love an animal unconditionally

PART ONE
NEW HAVEN

1

INFESTATION

The room was still dark when Jim Harden opened his eyes. He was glad it wasn't quite daybreak yet and was tempted to drift back to sleep when someone pounded on the cabin door.

"Jim? What's that noise?" Cynthia Lane said, nestled next to him under the covers.

"Someone's beating down our door." Harden threw off the heavy woolen blanket and climbed out of bed. He slipped on his trousers and donned a shirt.

Stepping out of the bedroom, he glanced over as another door opened.

Old man Nelson stood in the doorway, his scruffy gray beard and mussed shaggy shoulder-length hair making his head look like a scraggily wintry bush. He shot Harden a squinty-eyed look. "Must be damn important by the sound of it."

Harden marched barefoot to the front door, unlatched the bolt, and pulled it open.

"Oh thank God," a young woman said.

"Emily, what is it?" Harden asked, doing his best to tamper his irritation of being rousted out of bed so early in the morning. He could tell by the panicked look in her eyes that she was desperate.

"We need Cynthia right away. It's the children. There's something terribly wrong with them."

"Just a minute and I'll—" but then Harden stopped when he heard Cynthia bolt out of the bedroom. She had thrown on some clothes and was in her stocking feet.

"Let me grab my kit," Cynthia said, having overheard Emily Waters' plea for help and rushing back into the bedroom.

She came out with a black medical bag and hurried to the front door. "Jim, would you please wake up Darren. I might need him." Her eighteen-year-old son often assisted Cynthia, once a registered nurse in her previous life and the only medically trained person for the twenty people living in the

New Haven encampment tucked away in an undisclosed location in the middle of the Canadian wilderness.

"I'll get the boy," Nelson said and slammed the heel of his hand a few times on the wall, which elicited a muffled response from inside the adjacent room.

Cynthia slipped on her boots by the door and shrugged into her coat while Harden did the same. He grabbed a flashlight hanging from a lanyard on a hook, but when he went to turn it on, the bulb flickered and he had to strike the base of the aluminum casing with the palm of his hand a few times to get the light to turn on properly.

"Let's go," Harden said, shining the beam on the ground as they traipsed across the spongy ground sodden from the fat dewdrops cascading off the branches of the tall spruce trees all around them in the early morning chill. They made their way past the other cabins, through the lingering wood smoke haze from the smoldering chimneys.

Emily ran ahead to the cabin farthest from the other structures and opened the door for Cynthia and Harden.

A single lantern was on a long table in the center of the room, casting an amber glow on the five cots butted against one wall. Harden saw Debra Stevens knelt beside one of her ailing children. Debra and Emily were recent widows after their husbands had been killed by a couple of murderous camp renegades, who were no longer a threat as they too were dead.

Debra turned when Cynthia came in. "I'm so sorry, this is all my fault. I should have come to you sooner."

"Are they all sick?" Cynthia asked.

"Yes, but each one is different. My boys are complaining of headaches and sore throats and the girls keep throwing up."

Cynthia looked at Harden. "Jim, could you turn up that lantern so I can examine them?"

Harden walked up to the table and opened the control valve so more fuel could feed the wick. The room brightened, so much that a couple of the kids flinched from the glare and lifted their blankets over their faces. He glanced over at Emily who was sitting on a bench with her son, Danny, on the other side of the room. The six-year-old boy seemed worried about his playmates but didn't appear to be ill.

Darren arrived and rushed in. "Do you know what's wrong with them?"

"Not yet. Jim, I could use some more light over here."

Harden picked up the lantern and held it up as he came over. He watched as Cynthia pulled back a blanket from the oldest Stevens boy. He was shivering so violently, the child's teeth were clicking together like ice cubes rattling in a glass. Harden noticed the boy's hands and his bare feet were covered with red blotches. "That looks like a nasty rash. Are those welts?"

"Blood blisters," Cynthia responded. She glanced over at Darren.

He had just pulled the covers off the other boy. "This one has it too."

"They all do," Debra Stevens confessed, holding back the tears. "At first, I thought it was poison ivy and I could treat it with some lotion we had that you had given us a while back. But it didn't seem to help. And then they all started getting sick."

"Mom," Darren said. "Take a look at this."

Cynthia stepped toward the other boy's cot.

"What is it?" Harden said, swinging the lantern for a closer look.

"It's a tick," Cynthia replied. "Emily, please help Debra check the other children, especially their scalps."

After completing a thorough visual examination of the children, it was confirmed that each child had anywhere from two to five ticks embedded in their skin.

"First thing we need to do is remove the ticks," Cynthia said. She reached into her kit and took out two sets of tweezers. She handed a pair to Darren. "Remember how I taught you. Grasp the body as close to the skin as possible and slowly pull upward. Whatever you do, don't break off the head or it will become infected."

"Don't worry, I got this," Darren replied.

Harden watched as the two women pointed out the ticks to Cynthia and Darren. It took almost three-quarters of an hour before all the embedded parasitic arachnids were completely extracted, and not a minute too soon for Harden, as his arm felt like it was about to fall off from the weight of the lantern, which he returned to the table.

Cynthia and Darren had moved to a corner of the room to discuss the children's condition far enough away so as not to be overheard by either Emily or Debra. After a moment,

Cynthia motioned to Harden that they should leave. Darren stayed behind to attend to the children.

Harden and Cynthia stepped outside. They walked over and stood under the dawn sunlight filtering down through the forest canopy.

"So how bad is it?" Harden asked.

"They have Rocky Mountain Spotted Fever."

"They'll live, right?"

"Only with a heavy dose of antibiotics," Cynthia said. "Without it, they'll die."

2

COMING UP SHORT

While walking back to get the medicine for the children, Harden and Cynthia greeted a few of the early risers stepping outside of their cabins to start their morning routines. A man wearing a sidearm came out to fetch an armful of firewood, while another man gave them a nod as he strolled out to the latrine in the woods.

It was not always an easy task being the camp leader when the men Harden was supposed to govern were not exactly model citizens as they all had criminal backgrounds and were hiding out in New Haven to elude the authorities.

There were only a handful of people in the camp Harden truly trusted even though everyone had vowed their allegiance.

"I wish we knew if Heflin was ever coming back," Cynthia said.

Bush pilot Tyler Heflin was the camp's only connection to the outside world and source of critical supplies.

"It's been over two months now," Harden said. "Somehow, I don't believe we'll be seeing him."

"You don't think it has anything to do with McFarland?"

"What, that he put a bullet in Heflin once they got to wherever it was they were going so he didn't have to share his stash of the money he stole from everyone here?" Harden knew Connor McFarland, who had once reigned over New Haven, was ruthless enough to do anything to cover his tracks after leaving the encampment on Heflin's floatplane.

"Or maybe they crashed and are both dead."

"Guess we'll never know," Harden said, opening the door to their cabin for Cynthia as they went inside.

Nelson was sitting at the table, drinking his coffee. "So what was the sudden emergency?"

"The Stevens kids are very sick," Cynthia replied.

"Damn," Nelson said. "Nothing serious I hope."

"They should be okay once they're treated with antibiotics."

Harden followed Cynthia to the open closet space where they kept their firearms, ammunition, extra bedding, and most importantly, a five-shelf metal rack reserved for medical supplies, the dwindling inventory sparse with two shelves completely bare.

Cynthia went methodically down the shelves, rummaging through the less than one hundred plastic bottles of medicines and boxes of first aid supplies until she reached the bottom shelf. "Where the heck is it?"

"Something wrong?" Harden asked.

"We're missing some inventory."

"Was it marked off from the list?"

Cynthia grabbed the clipboard hanging on the side of the rack. She perused the front page and then flipped to the second page. "No. This is so strange. I don't understand."

"What's missing?" Harden pressed.

"All of the hydrocodone."

Harden knew it was an opioid and quite addictive if abused and was the only drug they had as a painkiller, having run out of morphine. "You don't think Darren gave some out and didn't tell you?"

"He would never do that. He knows we have strict rules when dispensing medication."

"Well, grab a box of the tetracycline and we'll sort it out later."

"That's the problem," Cynthia said. "There is no more, that's gone as well."

3

PLAYED

Harden and Cynthia were about to go back to the women's cabin to talk with Darren when Cynthia's son saved them the trip.

"What's been keeping you?" Darren asked, coming through the door.

"What happened to the hydrocodone and tetracycline?" Cynthia said.

"What do you mean? There should be some boxes on the second shelf."

"They're all gone."

"That's impossible. They were there yesterday when I did the inventory." Darren marched over to the supply shelves and looked for himself. "You're right." He looked down at the check off sheet on the clipboard in his mother's hand. "See," he pointed, "I marked them down."

"So where did they go?" Harden asked.

"I have no idea."

"Were you here all day yesterday?"

"I was here the entire day just like you asked me. Mom, are you sure you didn't take the tetracycline with you when you and Jim went out to check on that homesteader complaining of stomach pain?"

"No," Cynthia replied. "I would have noted it on the inventory list if I had. Besides, it turned out he only needed a laxative."

"Where were you?" Harden asked Nelson.

"Supervising the work on the latrine," Nelson replied. "Why?"

"I was wondering if you might have seen anyone around the cabin."

"There was someone," Darren piped in.

"Who?"

"Cliff Baxter. He brought his woman with him."

"Darren!" Cynthia snapped, "Don't refer to Baxter's girlfriend as 'his woman.'"

"Why, that's what he calls her," Darren said in his own defense.

Harden sat on the edge of the table and crossed his arms. "So what did he want?"

"He said his..." Darren paused and looked at his mother, "his *girlfriend* wasn't feeling well and was complaining of a terrible headache. If there was something I could give her. I could tell by the look on her face she wasn't feeling well."

"So what did you do?"

"I went to the supply shelf to get her some aspirin."

"And where were they?" Harden asked.

A troubled look came over Darren's face. "I know, you tell me never to let anyone in the cabin without your say so, but she looked like she was about to pass out, so I let her sit at the table."

"And where was Baxter while all this was going on?"

"Standing beside her."

"Go on," Harden said.

"Well, I was about to get the aspirin when she let out this moan and fell onto the floor. I didn't know what was happening. She started twitching and I thought she was having a seizure. I tried calming her down, afraid she might swallow her tongue. I was trying not to panic."

"And what was Baxter doing while all this was happening?" Harden asked.

"I don't know. I was too distracted helping her."

Cynthia looked at Harden. "That must have been when Baxter snatched the hydrocodone and tetracycline."

"So why is it that this is the first we're hearing of this?" Harden asked Darren.

"She snapped out of it and said her headache was gone. Besides, I knew you would be angry with me for letting them in the cabin. So I didn't say anything. I had no idea they had played me so they could steal the medicine."

Harden glanced over at Nelson. "What do you think?"

"Baxter always struck me as a dopehead. Probably plans to keep the opioids for himself and trade the antibiotics to the homesteaders."

"We have to stop him before he does," Cynthia said, "or those kids will die."

"Let's hope we're not too late," Harden said, walking over to the storage space where they kept their cache of weapons, to get his gun.

4

THE YURT

Cynthia and Darren stood in the doorway of the cabin as Harden and Nelson began to head out. "Are you sure you don't want us to come along?" Cynthia asked.

"You two better stay here, just in case there's trouble," Harden replied. He was wearing his gun belt with his Browning semi-automatic holstered on his hip. He felt confident he could resolve the matter peaceably but wasn't going to take any chances. Besides, Nelson was coming along with his hunting rifle and if there was anyone Harden could rely on to have his back it was the old man.

"Be careful," Cynthia said.

"We will," Harden promised. Harden and Nelson walked through the clearing and followed the path into the trees. It didn't take them long before they passed the small cabin that used to belong to Clayton Sanders, the camp's miller, before he was viciously attacked and killed by a wild animal later believed to be a big cat. No one lived in the dwelling anymore as an aging spruce had uprooted and flattened the clapboard building to the ground.

They continued on for a mile or so until they reached a glade where there were remnants of a burnt structure, which at one time used to belong to a family before they managed to escape on Heflin's floatplane before the pilot inexplicably disappeared off New Haven's radar.

"That place was always unlucky," Nelson commented, acknowledging the charred rubble.

"You could be right." Harden had heard rumors of other people living there who had mysteriously gone missing and were presumed dead, buried somewhere out in the forest.

Harden drew his Browning from the holster and pulled back the slide, putting a round in the chamber and cocking the gun. He slipped the pistol back into the holster knowing if he had to draw the weapon it would be ready to fire with a pull of the trigger.

They hiked up the trail, and once on the crest of the hillock, gazed down at the round rotund roofed structure on a wooden platform foundation.

"Didn't that used to be the Malkowskis' place?" Nelson said.

"Not anymore," Harden replied. "Best stay alert from here on out."

"Yeah, Baxter can be one squirrely dude when he's high." Nelson threw back the bolt on his hunting rifle and rammed it forward, inserting a cartridge into the firing chamber. "Think it's just him and the woman?"

"We'll soon find out," Harden answered making his way slowly down the hillside.

As they approached, Harden studied the dwelling, which resembled a nomad tent, the underlying shape made of stressed poles and bowed lattice to form the circular shelter covered with weatherworn tarps and canvas. A narrow deck was in front of the main door and served as a porch area.

Harden saw a mangled patio chair lying on its side by the open door. "This doesn't feel right." Harden drew his handgun and held it down by his side. He stared into the dark doorway and yelled up, "Baxter! You inside?"

A few seconds passed and Harden called out again. "Baxter! If you're in there, come out and show yourself! We know you stole the medicine and want it back!"

Still there was no reply from inside the yurt.

Harden took the steps up to the narrow porch. He raised his gun and took a single step through the doorway. He could tell the place might have been a suitable habitat at one time but not anymore. The planked flooring was covered in dirt and mud and littered with clothes and bedding. Food-caked plates cluttered the table. The place had an unpleasant lingering stench of vomit and defecation.

Nelson came inside and scanned the room with the muzzle of his rifle. "I knew Baxter was a slob but this is ridiculous."

Harden saw a shape under a blanket on the floor. He crossed the room and pulled back the cover. "Jesus," he gasped when he saw the woman's pale face. He closed the lids over her sightless eyes. "I can't believe Baxter just left her like this."

"Son of a bitch," Nelson cursed.

"Look around for the medicine."

For ten minutes they kicked about the debris on the floor and sifted through the clothes, checking every possible hiding place, only to come up empty.

"He must have taken it with him," Harden concluded. "As we didn't see him on our way over here, he must have left by the back trail."

"What should we do about her?" Nelson asked.

"We'll deal with this later. First we have to get that medicine." Harden draped the blanket back over the dead woman.

Stepping outside, Harden made sure the door was securely shut to deter any animals from sneaking into the yurt while Nelson went down to look for any tracks.

"You were right, Jim. He went this way," Nelson said, looking up after studying the ground.

"Let's go find the bastard!"

5

ON THE EDGE

Having no idea how much of a head start Baxter had on them, Harden insisted they keep to a fast pace if they were to catch him before he got the opportunity to barter away the much needed medicine. Harden knew once a transaction was made, it might be too late and impossible to reverse.

Their pursuit soon took them into higher ground.

Crossing over a fast-moving creek, Harden could tell Nelson was starting to show signs of slowing down as he almost slipped on a slick, moss-covered boulder, struggling to jump to the opposite bank. "You okay, old man?"

"Just lost my footing there for a moment."

"How about I keep going and you catch up when you can?"

"How about you stop worrying about me," Nelson shot back.

Harden heard the rumbling of cascading water beyond the trees in the distance.

"How long do you think we have?" Nelson asked, doing his best to keep up as they hiked up a steep slope.

"What do you mean?"

"Before the DOJ decides to come back and settle the score. What were their names again?"

Harden had to think for a moment. "Higgins and Pierce." The two Department of Justice operatives had brought a team to arrest the residents of New Haven and bring them to justice, and would have succeeded if Ernie Mason and his fellow homesteaders hadn't intervened and foiled the mission.

"I mean it's been nearly two months," Nelson said.

"I'm aware."

"Don't forget they know who we are."

"I doubt we're high on their priority list."

"I wouldn't be so sure," Nelson said, and then grabbed Harden by the arm. "Up ahead, I think I saw something."

Harden glanced up through the trees and spotted Baxter standing on a granite ledge overlooking a waterfall crashing down onto boulders and feeding into a raging river.

Baxter spotted them coming and stepped back. He was holding a revolver in his right hand and a rucksack by the strap in his other hand.

"Try not to spook him," Harden whispered to Nelson.

"Stay back!" Baxter shouted, the heels of his boots precariously close to the edge of the cliff. "I swear I didn't kill her! I told her to slow down but she wouldn't listen."

"We're not here about your girlfriend. All we want is the medicine you took."

"You're lying!" Baxter yelled back.

"The bastard's high as a kite," Nelson said.

"Step away from the edge so we can talk," Harden said, trying his best to defuse the situation. "Just give us the drugs."

"Bullshit!" Baxter dangled the rucksack over the edge. "Leave me alone or I'll drop it. I swear!"

Harden rested his gun hand on the grip of his holstered pistol. "You don't want to do that!"

Nelson raised the muzzle of his rifle. "Let me take him down."

"Don't. You do and he'll go over for—" but Harden didn't get a chance to finish his sentence as Baxter brought up his gun and fired. Harden heard the bullet whiz by and saw Nelson jerk back as the slug punched into his shoulder. Nelson dropped his rifle and fell to the ground.

Afraid he would be next, Harden drew the Browning and shot Baxter in the chest. The man teetered back and plummeted over the edge.

"Aw shit!" Harden cursed, watching the man fall and crash onto the boulders below, the rucksack landing in the raging waters and drifting away. He turned to Nelson. "How bad is it?"

"I'll be all right."

"You sure?"

"Jim! Forget about me; get the damn medicine!"

Harden gazed down at the water and spotted the rucksack floating downriver.

He unbuckled his gun belt, letting it drop to the ground and raced down the path, cutting over to the embankment as he ran as fast as he dared, looking for the best way down, praying the rucksack stayed afloat long enough for him to retrieve it, that it might miraculously get snagged on a branch of a fallen tree, before his boots slipped out from under him and he took a thirty-foot head-dive into the turbulent waters.

6

DIGGING DEEP

Cynthia was on her way back to her cabin when she was surprised to see Ernie Mason with a rifle slung over his shoulder and two homesteaders carrying Nelson, who was unconscious. "Oh my God, what happened?"

"He's been shot. We found him in the woods. Where do you want him?" Mason asked.

"This way." Cynthia directed them inside the cabin. "Sit him on the bench so I can take a quick look at the wound." The two men stood on each side of Nelson and sat him down. "Help me get his coat and shirt off," she further instructed. One man went to work disrobing Nelson's upper body while the other man propped him up.

"Anything you want me to do?" asked Mason, slinging the rifle off his shoulder and leaning the weapon up against the wall.

"Grab me some compresses off the shelf over there," Cynthia said, pointing across the room.

Mason went over, snatched a box, and came back. "Here," he said, taking out a large gauze.

Cynthia placed the pad over the gunshot wound to stop any further bleeding. "Who shot him?" she asked Mason.

"Don't know."

"You didn't see Jim out there?"

"No, just Nelson. Why?"

"They went out looking for Cliff Baxter. They were trying to retrieve medicine that Baxter stole."

"My guess it was Baxter shot Nelson," Mason said. "Want us to go look for Jim?"

"Would you mind?" Cynthia said.

"Not at all." Mason looked at his men. "Get Nelson situated on the table and I'll stay here to help out."

Once Nelson was positioned on the table, the two men left to go look for Harden.

Cynthia cleaned the blood from Nelson's shoulder the best she could so she could see the entry wound. She pressed the flesh around the bullet hole. "I can't say for certain but he might have a fractured clavicle. I'm going to need a sharp knife and some rubbing alcohol."

"Coming right up," Mason said. He went to the supply shelf and came back with a plastic bottle. He reached into one of the sheaths on his belt and pulled out a thin bladed knife with a sharp tip. Being an obsessive collector of anything to do with knives, Mason had abundant cutting tools that could be used for hunting, combat, culinary, and butchering, back at his cabin.

"Can you put some heat on it?" Cynthia asked.

"Sure." Mason went over to the stone fireplace where a few burning embers were still smoldering from the previous night. He tossed in some kindling and got the fire going again. He held the tip of the knife over the rising flame.

"I'm hoping he'll stay unconscious when I start digging around for the bullet but just in case he comes to, I want you to be prepared to hold him down."

"Not a problem. Here, I think it should be sterile enough," Mason said, holding the handle at the end so Cynthia could grip it without getting burned.

"Here goes." Cynthia worked the blade into Nelson's flesh and felt around for the piece of metal. Nelson let out a moan but didn't wake up.

"You better hurry," Mason warned, standing at the head of the table, placing one hand on Nelson's uninjured shoulder, the other on the man's chest.

"I found it," Cynthia said. She twisted the blade to get under the bullet and gradually plucked it out. "There." She poured alcohol into the wound and applied a large compress. Speckles of blood seeped through, so she taped on another dressing.

"If you want, I could help you get him into bed," Mason offered.

"Okay." Cynthia figured the old man couldn't weigh more than a hundred and fifty pounds and wouldn't be too difficult to move into the bedroom. Even though Mason was lean himself, he was notably strong. Together, they were able to get Nelson into bed without any trouble. Cynthia draped a blanket over Nelson. "There, he should be better after some bed rest."

They went out into the main room.

Cynthia collected the bloody compresses, threw them into the fireplace to burn, and began to clean up the table. "Thank you, Mason, for bringing Nelson."

"Couldn't exactly leave him out there to bleed to death, could I?" Mason quipped as he cleaned the blood off the knife Cynthia had used to dig out the bullet and slipped it back in the sheath on his belt.

"Seems we've been thanking you a lot lately. I mean, if it wasn't for you, I don't know what would have happened if you and your men hadn't showed up when you did."

"Guess we'll never know, now, will we."

"I sometimes wonder if maybe it would have been a good thing if they had taken the children away. At least then they would have had a chance of having normal lives and some kind of a future. Certainly not what they have here."

"You'd rather those government types had separated them from their mothers and put them in protective custody?" Mason said.

"At least they would have had access to proper health care. The Stevens kids are going to die and there is nothing I can do to save them," Cynthia snapped, trying her best to hold back the tears.

Cynthia heard the cabin door open and turned to see who it was.

Jim stood in the doorway. He had a bruise on his right cheek and a cut above his left eye. His damp hair was matted to his head, his clothes soaking wet and looked like a drowned rat but still managed a smile as he tossed a rucksack onto the table.

"Oh my God, Jim. You did it!"

7

TOUGH DECISION

Two days had passed and the children were showing signs of improvement once they had been put on a regiment of tetracycline. Cynthia had been overjoyed but knew it was only a matter of time before another medical emergency cropped up. She dreaded to think what would happen if there was no medicine left to get them through another crisis.

She was accompanying Harden on a stroll through the woods when she said, "I don't know how much longer I can do this."

"Do what?" Harden asked.

"Effectively treat everyone here. We've just enough tetracycline to get these kids through this and then that's it. Thanks to Baxter's little stunt, we're out of pain pills, which Nelson could really use right now."

"He's a tough old bird, he'll manage."

"You didn't have a bullet dug out of you."

"No, you're right, but I do know what it feels like being bounced about like a pinball in a raging river."

"Sorry," Cynthia said, knowing he had selflessly risked his life and could have drowned swimming downriver to retrieve the rucksack before it submerged in the swift flowing waters.

"For a second there I was beginning to feel a little under appreciated."

"We wouldn't want that." Cynthia stopped walking and drew Harden towards her, kissing him passionately. He held her so tight she swore she could feel his heart beating through their thick jackets—or was it her heart pounding anxiously in her chest?

Soon as their lips parted, Harden looked down at her and said, "You know I'm afraid things aren't going to get any better here medical-wise, seeing as we're cut off from the outside world."

"But what can we do?" Cynthia asked.

"I think I know someone that might be able to help us."

"Who?"

"Remember I told you about those people up at that abandoned weather station?"

"Weren't some of them shot by your men?"

"Ancient history," Harden said with a shrug. "Besides, those men are all dead. After all was said and done, I think Nelson and I drummed up a bit of friendship with those folks."

"Friends? Isn't that stretching it a little?"

"Maybe. It's not like we have many options. What do you think?"

"It's worth a shot. I'd like to go along," Cynthia said.

"No, you should stay here in case you're needed. Besides, the hike is through some pretty rough terrain. It could get dangerous."

"Who are you planning on taking? Nelson sure isn't in any condition."

"I'd rather he be here anyway."

"What about the other men?"

"I can't risk it. Some of them might get jealous when they see what these folks have and start some trouble. No, I think I would like to take Darren. I mean, he knows what medical supplies we need, that is if they're willing to part with any."

"What if someone should ask where you are?"

"Tell them I took Darren on a hunting trip."

"I don't know, Jim," Cynthia said. "He's just a boy."

"Cynthia. He's eighteen. It's time you thought of him as a man."

"How do you know he'll even want to go?"

"He'll go if he knows it'll help. I know he's fond of those children."

"You're right. Promise you won't let anything happen to him. You'll keep him safe."

Harden placed his hands on both her shoulders and looked her straight in the eyes. "I promise to keep him safe. So what do you say?"

"Okay, if you promise. So when will you leave?"

"Tomorrow morning just before dawn."

"Then we better get back to the cabin," Cynthia said, "and get you both packed."

8

DEPARTURE

Cynthia hadn't gotten much sleep worrying if maybe she should reconsider if Darren should even go. She'd half expected—or rather hoped—he would have refused to accompany Harden on what was surely to be a dangerous journey. But her son had jumped at the chance to go. Cynthia couldn't help feeling proud of her boy even though there was a part of her that feared he might never return.

"I think that's everything," Harden said, grabbing his backpack off the table and slipping on the shoulder straps.

Darren hefted his pack before putting it on. "This thing must weigh thirty pounds."

"Try forty. Better get used to it," Harden said.

Cynthia prayed he wouldn't be too tough on her son, knowing Harden wasn't the pampering type. Even though Harden was a compassionate person, it was also important he never exhibited any personal traits that might be misconstrued as a sign of weakness. With the exception of Nelson, who was Harden's trusted friend and considered by all to be second in command, there hadn't been anyone in the camp who showed any interest in challenging Harden for the seat of camp leader.

Nelson stepped out of his bedroom and joined the three standing at the table. His right arm was in a sling. He looked refreshed after some bed rest. "You two taking off?"

"Think you'll be able to hold down the fort, old man?" Harden asked.

"I might have a broken wing but I still got some pep in me."

"Glad to hear."

Darren shrugged on his backpack and tightened the belt around his waist. He grabbed both straps with his hands and adjusted the weight on his hips. "This isn't so bad."

"Tell Jim that after you've gone a few miles," Nelson grinned.

"How far is this weather station?" Darren asked Harden.

"A few days from here." Harden looked at Cynthia. "If you and Darren want to go outside and say your goodbyes, I'd like to have a word with Nelson before we leave."

"Sure, Jim. Come on, Darren. Let me give you a proper send-off." Cynthia put her hand on Darren's shoulder and guided him toward the door.

"Mom, you're not going to kiss me outside, are you? What if someone's watching?"

"Just keep marching. A mother's got a right to kiss her son if she wants to."

Once Cynthia and Darren had gone outside, Harden looked at Nelson. "You're sure you're up for this?"

"Stop your fretting." Nelson opened his sling wide enough for Harden to see the small revolver inside.

"Any trouble, you get Mason."

"I doubt I'll need him."

"Don't be too proud, old man."

"I hear you. What do I have to do, break a bottle of champagne over your bow to get you to leave?"

"Just watch over Cynthia."

"I will. You can count on me."

"I know."

"So how about you quit lollygagging," Nelson admonished. "If you haven't noticed, you're wasting daylight."

9

THE BIG REVEAL

Harden wasn't intentionally pushing the young man but he wanted to cover as much ground on the first day as possible and had been forging on for more than two hours without bothering to rest. Darren had stayed right behind Harden and never voiced a complaint. But when it stretched into the third hour, Harden decided there was no point in killing themselves and stopped to take a break.

"How are you holding up?" Harden asked Darren as they both took off their backpacks and found suitable seating on a couple of flat-surfaced rocks.

"Are we going to keep this pace the entire trip?"

Harden didn't want to say anything that might suggest he thought Darren might not be up to the rigorous hike and just gave the young man a thin-lipped grin. "Did you remember to wear two pairs of socks?"

"Just like you told me. The last thing I want is a boot full of blisters."

"While we're here, care for some coffee?"

"Sure," Darren replied.

"You make the fire."

Darren got to his feet and went about gathering up handfuls of dry moss, twigs for kindling, and some dry branches. He built a small teepee on the ground between two flat rocks. Creating sparks by striking a flint with the edge of his knife, he ignited the moss and soon flames were licking through the branches.

"Where did you learn to build a fire like that?" Harden asked as he poured water from a canteen into two tin mugs and put them close enough to the flame to heat up.

"Sure you won't laugh?"

"Got my word."

"The Boy Scouts."

Sometimes it was difficult for Harden to fathom that everyone living in New Haven had previous lives at one time, some more normal than others. He could only imagine the strain it must have been on Cynthia and Darren when they were suddenly uprooted by William Lane, a man that was supposed to be a loving husband and caring father but in reality was a diabolical physician that molested his patients, and had forced his family to flee the country before he was indicted and sentenced to life in prison.

Once the water had boiled, the two sat quietly and sipped coffee from their mugs.

"I know it's none of my business," Darren said, blowing the steam off his mug, "but you've never told us why you came to New Haven."

"Does it matter? I haven't even told your mother."

"Don't you think we have a right to know?"

Harden didn't want to lie though he feared the truth might inadvertently change their relationship.

Darren remained silent and sat patiently.

"I had a younger sister once. Her name was Gabrielle. Everyone used to call her Gabby because she was quite the talker."

"You said *used*."

"I'll get to that."

"Were you close?" Darren asked.

"Oh yeah. Even when she went off to college she would call me two or three times a week to see how I was doing." Harden put his mug down on the ground and rubbed his hands together. "One night, she was out with three of her college friends and their car was hit head-on by a drunk driver. None of them survived but the bastard in the other car walked away without a scratch. He was arrested and charged with four counts of vehicular manslaughter.

"I went to the courthouse on the first day of the trial thinking this guy was going to get what he deserved for killing my sister and it was a slam-dunk case. Seemed there was a major screw up. There was no record of this guy ever getting a Breathalyzer test. Sounded like bullshit to me. The judge gave the bastard six months community service."

"What you're saying is basically he walked free," Darren said.

"You might say that."

"That's not right."

"Later I learned the guy was tight with some very influential people and they must have tampered with the evidence."

"So what did you do?"

"It wasn't hard to find out where this creep lived. One night I waited outside his place for him to leave and followed him to this bar. He went inside and joined some friends at a booth in the back. I sat at the bar and watched them for about an hour. By then they were pretty drunk. I figured it was time to confront him and walked over. The guy looked up at me. I asked him how he felt knowing he had killed four innocent kids. He acted like he didn't know what I was talking about and told me to get lost.

"When I told him my sister had been in that car, he got this strange look on his face. That's when I took out my gun and shot him. I figured his friends had some part in the cover-up, so I killed them too."

Darren didn't know what to say and just stared at Harden.

"Make sure that fire is out before we leave," Harden said, relieved the big reveal was finally out on the table.

10

FIRST ENCOUNTER

Harden hoped he hadn't overplayed his hand telling Darren about how he had dealt with the man responsible for his sister's death. The young man didn't talk anymore on the subject as though the discussion had never happened, which was fine by Harden, for the time being. He knew sooner or later he would have to find a way to tell Cynthia. He surely didn't want her hearing how he had killed a group of men in cold blood from her own son.

They continued hiking for most of the day, taking breaks here and there, snacking on nuts, berries, and jerky they'd packed for the trip, figuring to have a proper meal when it came time to set up camp for the evening.

The journey so far had taken them up steep inclines and down rough terrain through the dense forest. They had reached a parcel of flat ground when Harden heard something up ahead moving about behind a large overgrowth of brush.

"Think it's a deer?" Darren asked, having heard it too and stopping when Harden put up his hand.

"Sounds bigger. More like an elk."

"What if it's a bear? Shouldn't we go another way?"

"Let's see what it is, then decide." Harden kept his rifle ready in case they had to defend themselves and crept towards the scraggly hedgerow. He crouched and did his best to part the branches without making too much noise. Darren knelt beside him and they peered through the opening.

"What the heck is that?" Darren said.

"I'm not sure," Harden replied.

The gray animal with rough skin grazing twenty feet away was the size of a cow, but didn't look anything like any bovine Harden had ever seen before. It had a knobby jut of bone above its flaring nostrils, downward horns covering each side of its thick-lipped mouth, and two calcium protrusions on the top of its forehead in front of a pair of spiky ears. It looked extremely powerful with its thick neck, muscular shoulders, and tree trunk legs.

They watched for a minute or two while the strange-looking creature continued to pull grass out of the ground with its teeth and loudly chewed.

Suddenly, without warning, a huge beast burst out from a stand of trees bordering the meadow.

"Run!" Harden yelled once he saw what it was. He grabbed Darren by the coat sleeve and yanked him to his feet as they bolted back into the forest. Harden didn't have time to process what he just saw, his adrenaline pumping as he ran despite the forty-pound pack slamming against his back, figuring if the young man sprinting in front of him could do it, so could he.

He heard the massive creature flattening saplings and crushing bushes, banging into trees, the beast snorting and billowing like a steam engine, the vibrations of its powerful hooves resonating up through the soles of Harden's boots every time they hit the ground.

Darren cut a zigzag path and Harden followed, slaloming through the thick tree trunks until they were certain the creature had given up the chase. They finally stopped and bent over, hands on their knees.

"What the heck was that?" Darren said, catching his breath.

"You're not going to believe it," Harden replied. "That was a rhino."

"What in the world is a rhinoceros doing out in the middle of the Canadian wilderness?"

"Your guess is as good as mine," Harden said.

"And what was that other animal?"

"I don't know. We best push on before it gets dark."

"I'm all for that."

11

CAMPFIRE CHAT

Harden figured they had traveled twenty-five miles despite having to make a detour after the close encounter with the territorial rhino by the time they finally set up camp. As before, when they had taken the short break earlier in the day for some coffee, Harden had let Darren prepare the fire while he set up the lean-to shelter under the low-hanging pine branches.

The smoke of the fire drifted up between the towering two hundred foot tall spruces looming over their campsite. There was enough of a break in the canopy to afford a spectacular view of the stars dotting the night sky high above.

"So what's for supper?" Darren asked, removing his boots and warming his feet by the fire.

"Something I like to call *Poor Man's Stew*. Some cut up carrots, potato chunks, a little flour and strips of venison with a dash of salt and pepper," Harden said, stirring the simmering concoction in the pot on the campfire. "If you go in my bag there should be some bread your mother packed for us."

Darren leaned over and opened the flap on Harden's backpack. He reached inside and took out a cloth bundle. He opened it up, revealing a large loaf of baked bread and after placing it on a tarp, cut off a couple of slices. He closed up the cloth and put the loaf back.

After the broth had thickened, Harden scooped two helpings of his stew into a couple of metal pans and handed one to Darren.

"Smells good," Darren said, inhaling the rising steam.

"Wait until you taste it." Harden spooned a large portion into his mouth then regretted it instantly when it burned his tongue. Rather than spit it out, he opened his mouth wide and let the air mingle with the food, cooling it enough so he could swallow. "You might want to give it a minute."

Darren looked at Harden and blew on his food. "I still can't stop thinking about that rhino."

"Yeah, I guess that's something you don't see every day."

"I'll say," Darren replied and took a bite of stew meat. "Hey, this *is* good."

"I imagine after hiking all day, anything would taste good right about now."

"No, I mean it. This is great."

"Glad you like it."

"Getting back to that rhino; any idea what it's doing here?" Darren asked.

"I have my suspicions."

"Does it have anything to do with where we're going?"

Harden took another bite of his food. He placed the metal pan on the ground and wiped his mouth with his sleeve. "Remember when our camp was attacked a while back?"

"You mean by those government agents?"

"No, not then, by the big cats."

"I know a lot of people died that night. I was inside the cabin when it happened."

"And what did your mom tell you?"

"The camp was attacked by mountain lions," Darren replied.

"They weren't mountain lions."

"Then what were they?"

"Sabertooth cats."

"No, that's impossible. They're extinct."

"Not anymore. I believe the people at the North Star Weather Station have something to do with it. When Nelson and I were there we saw plenty of surveillance equipment and computers. They're running some kind of science project and it has nothing to do with the weather. There's something else I should mention," Harden said.

"What's that?"

"There's a primitive tribe living with them."

"What, like Inuts?" Darren said, ready to shovel another spoonful of food into his mouth.

"No, not Eskimos. A prehistoric clan of warriors."

12

RITE OF PASSAGE

Cynthia woke up to the tantalizing aroma of coffee brewing. She got out of bed and put on some clothes. Stepping out of the bedroom, she found Nelson sitting at the table. He had poured her a cup. "Morning."

"Morning," Nelson replied.

"Where's your sling?" Cynthia asked, sitting in the chair next to the old man.

"Don't need it." Nelson demonstrated by raising his arm at shoulder height.

Even though Nelson didn't grimace, Cynthia could see it in his eyes he was having a bit of pain. "You're not fooling me. You really need to let yourself heal properly."

"I don't want them seeing me walking around with that damn sling. Might give them ideas, if you know what I mean."

"Wish there was something I could give you," Cynthia said.

"I'll live. How are the kiddies doing?"

"Just like you, they'll live thanks to Jim."

"I bet he's wishing—" Nelson stopped when there was a loud knock at the cabin door. "Who the hell is that?"

Cynthia got up from the table and went across the room. She opened the door and saw Orson Terrell and Craig Hoskins standing outside. They looked like a couple of militants with their heavy beards, camouflage jackets, and trousers tucked inside their black shin-high laced military-style boots, Terrell carrying a short barrel combat shotgun, Hoskins with an M4 carbine.

"Need to talk to Harden," Terrell said.

"Jim's not here," Cynthia replied.

"Where is he?"

Cynthia hesitated for a moment. "He took my son hunting."

"When will they be back?" Terrell wanted to know.

"Maybe a day or two. I can't really say for sure."

"Why so long? There's plenty of game around here."

"If you must know Jim thought it would be good if he and Darren spent time alone together."

The two men looked at one another.

Hoskins let out a laugh. "You mean like some rite of passage bullshit?"

"That's right," Cynthia replied.

"Why all the questions?" Nelson said, joining Cynthia in the doorway. "Is there a problem?"

"Nothing that concerns you," challenged Hoskins.

"Don't forget I'm in charge when Jim is away," Nelson said, glaring at the men.

Knowing she had to defuse what was becoming an increasingly confrontational situation, Cynthia sidestepped in front of Nelson and said, "What is it you men want?"

"We're not happy with the living arrangements," Terrell said.

"Oh, and why's that?"

"The women. There're two of them and eight of us."

"Your point?"

"A man has his needs, if you know what I mean," Terrell said.

"Not fair you ask me, pretty things like that and no man to speak of," Hoskins said.

"No one's asking you," Nelson snapped. "Rules are rules. What do the other men say?"

Terrell just shook his head. "What do you think?"

"If you haven't forgotten, Emily and Debra are both widows. *Grieving* widows, I must add," Cynthia said. "And as far as I can see, neither one of you are what you would call perspective husband material."

"Who said anything about wanting to be a husband?" Hoskins said. "Just seems a waste them living all alone in that cabin."

"Don't forget they have children," Cynthia reminded them.

"Let me get this right," Nelson said. "You two thought you'd just waltz over here and Jim was going to give you his blessing?"

"Something like that," Terrell said.

"Get the hell out of here."

"If I were you I'd watch your back, old man," Hoskins said.

"Leave, and I better not hear you've been pestering those women."

Cynthia was half expecting Terrell and Hoskins to raise their gun muzzles and point their weapons but instead they stepped back and walked away. She looked at Nelson. "We could be in for some trouble."

The old man nodded. "You can bet this isn't over by a long shot."

13

GONE ROGUE

Four thousand miles away, Special Agent Kevin Higgins was climbing the marble staircase in the Department of Justice building to the second floor. Stepping into the archway, he found the mahogany door open leading into the reception area. A secretary with grayish-brown hair looked up from her desk and smiled. "He's expecting you."

"Thanks," Higgins said. He opened the door and went inside.

"Kevin," Assistant Attorney General Jonas Higgins greeted, "how is my favorite nephew?"

"Last I checked you only have one."

"That is true. Have a seat."

Higgins sat in the chair facing his uncle's desk.

"I take it you're well rested?"

"To be honest, I wasn't expecting to be on leave for so long."

"I figured you could use some serious time off."

"A guy can go a little batty after two months."

"I'm sure he can. Anyway, I wanted to welcome you back."

"Thank you, sir. I hope I didn't embarrass you."

"I have to admit I was expecting a different outcome. At least you were able to come home safely. It would have been nice if you had been able to bring back the tablets your team had used to fingerprint and photograph the suspects. Good you have a thing for faces and were able to identity some of them from our database. Unfortunately, no one was on our top ten most wanted, though it doesn't mean they're not out there. I called you here because there has been a new development."

"Oh, and what's that?"

"It appears Bruno Pierce was humiliated and having trouble accepting defeat, especially after he and his men were stripped of their weapons and sent home with their tails between their legs. After I read in your report Pierce ordered his men to brutally ambush the survivalists without giving them the opportunity to surrender, I raked him over the coals and told him his conduct was unacceptable. He went into a rage and vowed he would get revenge. I told him to either resign or I would end his career."

"So what did he decide?"

"That's the thing. He seems to have disappeared. I'm worried he's gone rogue and is contemplating an unsanctioned assault on New Haven. We could be looking at a bloody massacre."

"There are women and children there."

"I'm well aware. I hate to think if this leaked out and the press got a hold of it. It wouldn't look good for the department. Which is why I'm sending you to stop him."

PART TWO
NORTH STAR
WEATHER STATION

14

MORNING ROUTINES

Dr. Tonya Mead took a moment to tidy up the sleeping quarters in the back room of the modular home. The rear wall had been recently repaired and the hewn boards did not match the undamaged walls provided in the tiny house building kit, but Tonya didn't care much for aesthetics, just as long as it kept the heat in and the draft out.

She stepped into the main room originally thought would be the laboratory but after some consideration, the embryologist decided the primary objective was animal management instead of further repopulating prehistoric creatures synthetically, especially when they were capable of procreating naturally on their own.

Which is why most of the equipment was still in boxes under a couple of long benches shoved against one wall.

Tonya passed through the den, which consisted of a futon couch, an ottoman, a handmade coffee table, two end tables with oil lamps, and four handcrafted chairs with thick cushions where she liked to relax most evenings and read.

Tonya heard her husband in the galley-style kitchen.

Sterling was standing at the sink. He turned and gave her a smile. "Hungry?"

"I can wait," Tonya said. She went up and kissed Sterling on the cheek while he twisted the cap on a thermos.

"That's okay, I packed some food," he said, "and we have coffee."

"Ready to head out?" Tonya asked, shrugging on her heavy parka.

"Yeah," Sterling replied. He stuffed the thermos inside a daypack and slipped the strap over his coat sleeve onto his shoulder. He reached in his jacket pockets, took out his gloves and stocking cap and put them on.

They stepped out onto the porch overlooking the majestic view of the Canadian forest stretching as far as the eye could see to the next snowcapped mountain range.

The sky was an icy glacier blue with lateral wisps of white cottony clouds.

"Brrr!" Tonya said, as the crisp high-altitude air chilled her lungs.

Sterling led the way down the steps. The ground crunched under their boots as they turned left and walked between the modular and the Quonset hut and its shed on their right, the thoroughfare a much-appreciated windbreak whenever it stormed heavily but today was just a nippy breezeway.

A burly bearded man and an attractive middle-aged woman both wearing woolen caps and donned in thermal coveralls stood at the entrance of a walk-in tunnel-type greenhouse dusted with snow just beyond the two buildings.

"Good morning," Tonya cheerily greeted Max and Janelle Malkowski.

"Getting an early start, I see," Max said.

"Looks like we're not the only ones," Tonya replied, noting the produce crate at Janelle's feet, already containing an abundance of freshly picked vegetables.

"Wanted to salvage what I could before the frost ruins everything," Janelle replied.

"How is the solar panel work coming along?" Sterling asked Max.

"Just waiting for Grant."

Tonya looked over at the shiny black rectangular panels mounted on the pyramid-shaped twenty-foot tall trestle tower situated a short distance away near the amphitheater base of the rocky cliff face stretching up to the snowcapped summit.

"Speak of the devil," Max said.

Tonya turned and saw Grant Olsson and Gale Vincent walking in their direction, having left the radio shack Grant had converted into their home, nestled back in the trees.

Trotting beside them was Sasha, Grant's two-hundred-and-fifty pound dire wolf.

"Hey, guys!" Gale called out. She was petite, much shorter than the strapping caretaker who looked like a lumberjack in his heavy plaid shirt, jeans, and hobnailed boots.

The group of friends headed toward the back steps leading up to the porch area of the Quonset hut. Tonya spotted Morgan Smith standing in a patch of snow by one of the three dune buggies, inspecting the battery under the uplifted driver's seat.

Tonya nudged Sterling's arm.

"Is there a problem?' her husband asked Morgan.

"Not as long as we don't plan on driving too far today," Morgan replied. "The batteries are only a third charged."

"That's not good," Sterling said. "What does that give us, thirty miles one way and back?"

"Something like that," Morgan replied.

"Don't worry," Grant said. "Max and I should have the charging stations up and running at a hundred percent by today."

"Oh, you will, will you?" Gale said.

"With your help, of course," Grant answered back.

Tonya knew Gale had no problem giving Grant a hard time for taking the credit when it was she who had originally rewired the Quonset hut and installed a charger control panel and the two 125 amp batteries that provided the electrical power for the outpost. A task the biologist accomplished without any previous electrical background by merely consulting the technical manuals. Max had been instrumental in upgrading the system, as he had once been an aeronautical engineer.

"Hey, worse comes to worst, you can always saddle up," Grant joked, motioning to the zebra-striped hipparion horses, each animal no taller than five feet at the shoulders, grazing in the corral next to the lean-to not far from the edge of the trees.

"By saddle up, you mean ride bareback," Tonya said. "No thanks."

The back door opened. Christian Manning stepped out carrying a walking stick, followed by his chocolate Labrador, Digger. The man had on a heavy pea coat, woolen trousers and hiking boots. A wide-brimmed hat covered his head.

"Morning, Christian," Tonya said. She reached down and gave Digger a pat on the shoulder. The dog responded with a vigorous tail wag.

"Morning, folks. Digger and I are going to take a morning stroll. If it's okay, I thought I might stay here today. I have some bones I would like to catalog."

Tonya thought it was hilarious the paleontologist was still obsessed with studying fossils when there were actual prehistoric creatures roaming the countryside not too far from where they lived. "Where are Finn and the others?"

"They're all inside sitting around one of the terminals like it's an episode of Animal Planet," Christian said, heading down the steps with Digger right behind.

Max and Grant went over to the trestle tower while Janelle carried her crate of vegetables inside. Sasha followed Christian and Digger as they went off on their walk.

"We should review the footage from last night," Sterling said. "Look for any animals in distress."

Tonya knew Sterling was compassionate about the animals released into the wild and feared for their safety, being an exotic veterinarian, and was often conflicted he was partially responsible for creating some of the most deadliest predators on the planet.

Sterling held the door for Tonya and Gale as they all went inside.

Much of what was in the Quonset hut had been abandoned by the meteorologists who previously occupied the weather station such as the lockers, desks, various cabinets and tables, and the many bunks lined up along the two curved walls.

New were the computers and surveillance monitors that captured the camera images of the animals' goings-on in the surrounding wilderness.

Tonya walked past a row of lockers and stopped when she noticed Sterling staring at the parietal artwork on the sloping wall that resembled an ancient storyboard one would expect to find deep within a long forgotten cavern.

She watched Sterling gaze across the room at the opposite wall, which was mostly blank except for the brushstrokes of a beginning tale. "Looks like Maya is back at it again. Good for her."

Tonya heard a yell and saw Finn jump up from a desk where the rest of the Paranthropus tribe was huddled in front of a surveillance monitor like a family sitting in front of the television set, watching their favorite show.

Gathered next to Finn were his mate, Jasmine, and Ash and Luna, the youngest of the women, Maya, and the two toddlers, Little Rook and Kelly. They seemed normal enough physically except for their ape-like facial features and the fact that the men were only five feet tall, the women a few inches shorter.

Finn, the tribal leader, and Ash wore animal skin togas while Jasmine, Luna, Maya, and the children were dressed in outfits Gale had fashioned from old garments she had found in a locker left behind by the crew of the weather station.

Tonya and Sterling walked over to see what all the excitement was about.

Finn looked at Tonya and pointed at the monitor, "Big cat kill!"

On the screen, a massive sabertooth cat had taken down a giant buck with twelve-foot span antlers and was in the process of savagely disemboweling its prey.

Even with all the chatter and noise, Tonya could hear Sterling let out a groan.

15

MORTAL COMBAT

Sterling strapped himself in the front passenger seat of the Utility Task Vehicle while Tonya climbed in the backseat and Morgan got behind the wheel. In the event of trouble, Morgan wore a sidearm and a long blade survival knife and there was a 12-guage Remington pump mounted between the front bucket seats.

"Where to?" Morgan asked, starting up the electric motor.

"How about we swing by the lake. I want to check on that herd." Lately, Sterling had been keeping tabs on seven mastodons that could usually be found foraging on woody vegetation under the pine trees bordering the shoreline.

Morgan spun the dune buggy around, sped past the Quonset hut, and headed down a well-traveled pathway through the forest. As always, Morgan drove like he was competing against phantom competitors in a cross-country race. Asking him to slow down was like convincing a scrupulous boxing champion to pull his punches.

Knowing Morgan was an excellent driver didn't sway Sterling from grabbing the tubular side of the roll bar and clutching on like his life depended on it. Some things you never got used to. Sterling glanced over his shoulder and saw the look on Tonya's face and knew she was thinking the same thing—*Slow the hell down, Morgan!*

The fat balloon tires cushioned much of the bumpy ride, occasionally leaving the ground a few times when the dune buggy went airborne, landing on the frozen ground with a bone-jarring jolt.

After covering what Sterling estimated was a ten-mile jaunt, he was relieved to see the flat surface of the crystal blue lake when they exited the woods.

That is until he saw two male mastodons facing-off in mortal combat, battling it out with their four-foot long tusks locked together, heads down and shoving belly-deep in the water.

The short-haired elephants stood about seven-feet at the shoulders. Sterling figured each one had to weigh somewhere in the vicinity of six tons.

Morgan drove the buggy onto the pebbled beach and skidded to a stop. "I don't think I've ever seen them fight before."

"They must be challenging each other over a female," Tonya said from the backseat. "They act this way when their testosterone levels spike. It's called *musth.*"

Sterling saw bloody gashes where they had gored one another, possibly cracking some ribs or worse, puncturing vital organs and causing internal bleeding. If they weren't separated they would kill each other or eventually grow tired and collapse. Even if they didn't drown, they would remain entangled on their sides and surely become easy prey for the nighttime predators. "We have to break it up before they further injure themselves."

"Are you out of your mind?"

Tonya jumped out. "Sterling's right. We have to do something."

"You want me to go over there and referee? Tell them to go back to their respective corners?" Morgan scoffed, getting out of the buggy.

"I've got a better idea," Sterling said. "Do we have any rope in the back?"

"Yeah, there's a good fifty feet in the utility box."

Tonya looked at Sterling. "Don't tell me you expect to lasso them."

"That's exactly what I'm thinking of doing." Sterling opened the metal box in the cargo bed and took out the coil of rope. He made a loop at one end and fed the rest of the rope through the hole to form a lariat.

"So what's the plan?" Tonya asked.

"I'm going to get as close as I can and see if I can get this rope around one of their tusks. When I do, Morgan should be able pull them apart with the buggy."

"That's your plan?" Morgan said skeptically.

"Got a better one?"

"Better tie the other end onto the back bumper nice and tight."

Sterling fastened the rope and sat on the end of the cargo bed while Morgan and Tonya climbed back into the buggy.

Morgan started up the motor. He drove slowly toward the edge of the bank and got as close as possible to the sparring pachyderms already showing signs of fatigue as they stumbled into each other.

At the edge of the forest, the rest of the herd—three females, a young adult male and a mastodon calf—paid little attention to the altercation. They were too engrossed scooping up twigs and leaves with their snouts and raising the aggregate food source up into their mouths with their trunks.

The battling beasts continued to tussle and bump heads.

Sterling jumped off the cargo bed. He held the lariat above his shoulder and waded knee-deep into the water. He made sure not to get too close in case the big animals staggered his way and crushed him. So far, they had been too engaged in impressing the females to pay any attention to the unimposing man standing only twenty feet away.

"Sterling, be careful!" Tonya called out from the water's edge. She had gotten out of the buggy so there would be less weight to burden the motor.

"Whenever you're ready!" Morgan shouted.

Knowing he probably wouldn't get a second chance, Sterling steadily approached, waiting for the precise moment and flung the looped rope at the pointed end of one of the tusks. It looped over the pointy end of the ivory. Sterling yanked back on the rope and cinched it tight. "Take it away!" he yelled.

Morgan drove slowly to take up some of the slack then tromped on the accelerator. The big balloon tires kicked up loose rock as the dune buggy sped off in the opposite direction of the feuding mastodons.

The rope snapped taut with a twang and yanked back the head of one of the mastodons, freeing its tusks but also pulling it off balance. The giant creature splashed into the water, narrowly missing Sterling, forcing him to scramble for shore.

Now free, the other pachyderm bounded out of the lake to rejoin the herd while the lassoed elephant struggled to its feet.

Sterling looked over his shoulder and saw the mastodon charge after him, the rope still looped round its tusk.

The front end of the dune buggy rose in the air as the vehicle did a wheelie on its back tires and flipped upside down with Morgan strapped in his seat.

Running for his life and unable to stop, Sterling was horrified to see the overturned vehicle dragged into the deep end of the water and quickly submerge with only the four balloon tires visible on the surface.

16

CHRISTIAN GOES FOR A STROLL

Christian never worried about venturing out in the wilderness as long as he had Digger by his side. The Labrador retriever was big for his size, weighing around one-hundred-and-twenty pounds. His head alone was as large as a watermelon. Christian knew the dog would never back down from a fight and had even faced-off once with a sabertooth cat and a lioness. It didn't diminish his valor that both animals had been near starvation and were too weak to put up much of a fight.

Having Sasha along was an added bonus of protection even though she preferred to wander off and explore, luring Digger away from Christian as the dog liked to tag along with the dire wolf. It wasn't unusual for the two to disappear for short periods of time leaving Christian by himself.

Much like now.

He was confident if he whistled loud enough, Digger would respond and come running.

Christian loved his somewhat solitary hikes through the forest even though this morning it was exceptionally cold. He looked up through the towering trees and saw a flotilla of gray storm clouds in the darkening sky.

He could hear the babbling creek he often visited a short distance away. Most often he would take different routes hoping to discover some bones he could bring back and analyze, even if they were only skeletal remains of a most recently killed animal.

Walking through a patch of waist-high ferns, Christian came to a fallen spruce tree blocking his path. The trunk was at least eight feet in diameter. The barrier was too high with its splayed branches for him to climb over. He looked down the length of the tree to his left and saw the tapered top, turned to his right and saw the mound of dirt surrounding the massive hole where it had uprooted. The damn thing had to be over two hundred feet long.

Christian wondered if Digger and Sasha had come this way, and if they had, which direction they had gone. He was about to call out to Digger when he heard an animal screech from where the tree had pulled out of the ground.

He heard more squealing creatures and walked along the length of the toppled tree, parting the ferns with his walking stick so as not to tread on something slithering in the underbrush that would not be as forgiving and bite back.

Christian gazed down into a five-foot deep impression in the overturned earth and saw a large litter of filthy piglets climbing over one another. They were hungry, crying for their mother, and if they didn't stop making such a racket they were going to attract every predator within hearing distance.

It was difficult to tell if they were feral pigs or warthog offspring. Whatever the parent, there was one thing he knew for certain.

It was never wise to get between a mother and her young.

Not if he didn't want to feel the wrath of an overprotective sow going hog wild and serving him up piecemeal to her brood.

Christian was about to turn around and retrace his steps when Digger began barking not too far away. Seconds later he heard the big dog crashing through the brush, most likely chasing after a rabbit.

Expecting to see a frightened hare race out, Christian was surprised to see Digger instead followed by a drove of stampeding wild pigs. They weren't after Digger; they were running for their lives.

Christian saw why when the gigantic beast charged out of the trees.

17

CHANGE OF WEATHER

Grant stood with Max under the open framework of the trestle tower. Two Canadian geese lay dead on the ground having broken their necks flying into the solar panels in the dark, their battered bodies covered with aluminum framing, smashed glass, and a shattered solar cell sheet.

"That's pretty much destroyed," Max said. "I'm going to have to reroute the junction boxes."

"Which means less power."

"I'm afraid so."

"Morgan's not going to like that," Grant said.

"I know."

Grant turned when he heard Gale step out of the rear door of the Quonset hut.

"I'm still waiting," she called out. "Figured out the problem yet?"

"Bird strike," Grant replied. "It's going to take us longer than we thought."

"Let me know when you need me," Gale said.

"Will do," Grant replied as Gale went back inside.

"I might be able to salvage some of this," Max said, grabbing the black plastic junction box that had snapped off of the back sheet of the panel upon hitting the ground.

Grant picked up the sections of aluminum frame and saw Max staring at the solar cell sheet, which had broken in half despite the protective encapsulant. "Maybe you could build a smaller panel."

Max looked over at Grant. "Some power is better than no power I suppose. Shouldn't take me more than an hour before we can install it."

A white flick passed by Grant's nose. He looked up and grumbled, "I can't believe it," when he saw a flurry of snowflakes drifting down through the metal beams.

Not only would the snowfall impede their progress in repairs it would also mean the heavy cloud cover would prevent the sun from radiating the panels and charging the solar batteries.

"I guess I'll have to work on this later," Max said, tucking the junction box in his coat pocket. "We better get cracking and rewire those panels." He opened his coat so he could access his toot belt and started climbing up the trestle tower.

"I'll be up to help you in a minute," Grant said. He picked up the two dead geese by their necks and carried them up the porch steps. Tossing the birds on the deck, he opened the door, and shouted, "Gale, I need you to come here!"

"Yeah, what is it? You guys can't be ready."

"No, but I have a nice surprise for you."

Gale came out and saw the dead geese. She yelled over her shoulder, "Janelle, come see this."

Janelle came to the door. "Oh my. Looks like we'll be having goose tonight."

"Sure does."

"I'll get Maya to help us with the plucking."

"I've got to get back and help Max."

"Did Finn talk to you?" Gale asked.

"No, about what?"

"The horses are almost out of food."

There wasn't natural grass for the horses to eat around the weather station as the ground was rock hard, so Finn and Ash had been forced to ride down to the valley to cut prairie grass and transport bales back on horse drawn sleds.

It was too dangerous to hobble the horses so they wouldn't run away while they were set out to graze because there were too many predators.

Grant and Max often helped out and took turns making runs with the dune buggies but then had to stop when problems arose with the charging stations.

"I'll go speak to him." Grant turned and went back down the steps. He looked up at Max clinging to a crossbeam with his arm tucked under a brace as he reran an insulated wire to reconnect two junction boxes. "I'll be right back. I need to talk to Finn."

"Take your time," Max replied. "This might be an easier fix than I thought."

Grant traipsed over to the corral. The falling snow was already sticking to the ground.

Finn was finishing up lashing a rope to two poles on either side of a horse's withers. A rawhide platform was draped between the two ten foot long shafts much like a Native American Indian travois. Ash was tightening the straps on a similarly rigged horse.

"Sure you don't want to wait?" Grant said, hoping to dissuade them.

"Horses need food," Finn replied.

"I know but there's a storm coming."

"Grant, come help," Ash said.

"I wish I could. The buggies are down and you know I can't ride." The hipparion horses were slightly bigger than Shetland ponies but too small to bear the weight of a full-grown man like Grant.

"Then we go," Finn said and mounted up.

"Hey, wait up!" Gale yelled, running over. She had a stocking cap pulled down around her ears and was wearing a down parka.

"Something wrong?" Grant asked.

"I haven't been able to reach Morgan on the radio."

"Maybe they're out of range."

"It's possible. Have you seen Christian?"

"He hasn't come back yet," Grant said.

"I'm starting to get worried. We need to find them and make sure they're okay."

"And how do you propose we do that without the buggies?"

"You can track Christian on foot. He can't have gone far."

"What about Sterling, Tonya, and Morgan?"

"Jasmine, Luna, and I will go look for them." Gale turned and waved the two Paranthropus women over. Jasmine and Luna were wearing their animal skin furs and foot coverings better suited for the harsh weather. They were armed with longbows and full quivers of razor-sharp, obsidian-tipped arrows.

Ash prepared the other horses.

Grant looked up at the blackening sky. The wind was picking up as the snow continued to fall. He wouldn't be surprised if they were looking at a full-blown blizzard.

The prehistoric men rode the packhorses toward the path leading down into the valley, while Gale, Jasmine, and Luna mounted the other horses and set out down the wide trail leading into the forest.

Grant walked back to the Quonset hut. He looked up at Max. The big man was perched on the same crossbeam, fiddling with a connector.

"Where's everyone off to?" Max asked, gazing down at Grant.

Grant took a moment to explain.

"Well then you better get a move on. I'll be okay here."

"Don't fall and break your neck."

"I'll do my best," Max replied.

Grant headed to the radio shack to grab his hunting rifle and snowshoes.

18

BOBBING FOR MORGAN

Tonya couldn't believe it when the dune buggy flipped upside down and was dragged into the lake. She thought for sure it would have been powerful enough to yank the rope off of the mastodon.

It only took seconds for the UTV to submerge.

Luckily, the balloon tires were buoyant and kept it from completely sinking.

There was no telling how long it would stay afloat or if Morgan could hold his breath as the mastodon towed the overturned vehicle across the lake twenty feet away from the shore.

Tonya hadn't noticed if Morgan had bothered to buckle up. For all she knew, he was disoriented and trapped under the water struggling to unsnap his harness.

Sterling was running a zigzag pattern on the opposite shore, hoping the looped rope would eventually slip off of the mastodon's tusk as the animal chased after him.

Whenever he veered to the right the rope became slack and dipped into the water and when he sprinted left, the wet rope snapped taut, pulling the dune buggy.

Tonya dashed into the shallows. She splashed waist-deep over to the inverted UTV and extended her arm under the water. She could feel the harness strapping Morgan in. She shook his shoulder but he didn't respond.

Reaching down she tried to undo his seatbelt buckle but the mechanism wouldn't release. Her only alternative was to cut the strap, so she fumbled around until she found Morgan's survival knife, thankfully still snug in its sheath. She pulled out the serrated blade and was about to cut the strap when the buggy jerked ten feet through the water causing her to lose her grip on the knife. She ducked under and retrieved the knife before it landed on the bottom.

She broke the surface and saw Sterling waving his arms. The mastodon had finally shaken off the rope and was lumbering for the forest.

"Come and help me get Morgan out!" she yelled to her husband.

Sterling bolted into the water. Tonya waded over to the buggy and quickly sawed through the harness. As soon as Morgan became free, Sterling and Tonya pulled him out of the rig. They grabbed their friend by the armpits and dragged him to shore. Tonya got right to work giving him chest compressions.

"Come on, Morgan," Sterling said, relieving Tonya. "Don't you die on us."

Morgan's eyes popped open just as a gush of water spewed out of his mouth and he began coughing. Sterling turned him on his side and patted him on the back so Morgan could expel whatever water was in his lungs.

"I guess that didn't go so well," Morgan said, spitting out more water.

Tonya spotted the small herd of mastodons congregating on the other side of the lake. The two large males that had been fighting before seemed to have reconciled and were grazing peacefully with the others. "Looks like they kissed and made up."

Morgan sat up and slowly got to his feet. He reached for his handgun but the holster was empty. "Damn," he said.

They watched the buggy drift ashore and settle on the rocks.

"Once we get it back on its wheels," Morgan noted, "it'll take a while to dry out the battery."

"Save us a good fifteen mile walk back," Sterling said.

"That's for sure," Morgan replied.

Tonya heard the trees rustling behind them. She turned and saw the stiff wind swaying the top branches. She looked up at a sky full of white. "Isn't this wonderful. It's starting to snow." She figured in the last thirty minutes the temperature had dropped twenty degrees.

"Great, just what we needed," Sterling said. "What now?"

"We have to salvage what we can from the buggy," Morgan said. "There's a water sealed survival kit in the cargo box with some foil emergency blankets. And some dry cartridges in the kit for the shotgun. Afterward, we can start a fire and get out of these wet clothes before they ice over."

"Either that or we turn into Popsicles," Tonya said, as she reluctantly waded back into the water with Sterling and Morgan.

19

ENTELODONT

The gigantic hell pig burst out of the forest with a boar's head in its mouth, and when it saw the other hogs scampering to get out of its way, the behemoth dropped the decapitated head on the ground to go after them.

The entelodont was a ferocious killing machine and big as a Clydesdale draw horse. It was a strange-looking beast with bone protrusions on both sides of a massive elongated head; huge bison hump shoulders on its shorthaired body tapering to a short-tailed rump and long powerful legs.

The most frightening features were its muscular curved flanged jaw and its chisel-shaped teeth, which could crush bone and rip the flesh and hides from even the largest of creatures in a matter of seconds as it wasn't afraid of anything.

Holding on to his walking stick, Christian grabbed Digger by the collar and dragged the dog behind the fallen tree away from the carnage. The paleontologist had never seen such savagery as the entelodont attacked one pig after the other, killing and mortally wounding the frantic swine in a grotesque slaughter fest.

The sow made the mistake of thinking she could protect her brood squealing in the dirt pit. The entelodont went after her next, crushing her skull with a horrendous head butt. With nothing to stop it, the hell pig leaned down into the pit and silenced the piglets one by one until they were all dead.

Christian knew there was no point in trying to outrun the murderous beast. He saw a large bough covered with a blanket of pine needles hanging down off the fallen tree trunk he thought might be a good place to hide.

"Come on, boy," he whispered. Christian held onto Digger's collar and crawled on his knees and one hand through the thick branches. Reaching the tree trunk, he sat upright with his back against the hard bark and draped his arm around Digger's shoulders, keeping his hand pressed firmly on the dog's chest.

Christian prayed the heavy pine scent of the tree would mask their smell and not attract the enormous pig.

Digger let out an anxious whimper.

"Quiet, boy," Christian said softly, rubbing the dog's chest to calm him down. He listened as heavy hooves approached.

A growl rumbled deep in Digger's throat.

"Shush."

A white speck fell through a narrow gap in the overhead branches and landed on Christian's coat sleeve. More snowflakes began to drift down through the pine needles.

Thunder boomed somewhere in the distance.

"Great," Christian said under his breath. "If things couldn't get any worse."

The entelodont shoved its ugly head into the branches, clacking its teeth but couldn't get any closer as its forehead was pressed up against the heavy bough.

Determined to get at Christian and his dog, the monstrous creature continued to bulldoze its way in. The timber cracked as the bough began to split.

Digger snarled and snapped at the giant pig while Christian used his walking stick as a spear and jabbed the beast in the face.

"Get back! Leave us alone!" Christian screamed, trying to poke out an eye, anything that would cause enough pain to make the hell pig give up its assault. He kept thrusting the walking stick, trying to stab the monster in the face.

The giant swine bit down on the staff and yanked it out of Christian's hands just as the bough broke in half.

But instead of attacking, the entelodont let out a screech and backed out of the branches. Digger pulled away from Christian and bolted out.

"Digger, no!" Christian got on his hands and knees and scampered through the large opening. "Oh my Lord!" he said when he saw Sasha attacking the entelodont from behind. The dire wolf had already inflicted a large gaping wound on the hell pig's thigh and was attempting to cripple the beast by biting its leg while Digger nipped at its face and shoulders.

The hell pig finally gave up, and with a prominent limp, staggered into the trees.

Sasha and Digger chased after to make sure it wasn't coming back and soon returned victorious, their faces covered in blood.

By now the snow was coming down heavily.

"Bravo, you two," Christian said. He gazed at the dead pigs scattered about the snow-covered ground and was tempted to take a small one back to the outpost.

But as they were feral, he didn't know what diseases they might be carrying. It wasn't worth running the risk of possibly infecting everyone at the outpost with the roundworm parasite trichinosis, which if not treated properly, could prove to be fatal.

"We should be getting back." Christian was surprised Digger and Sasha were no longer there and had snuck off. "Not again," he muttered. He took a moment to get his bearings, then raised the collar on his pea coat, pulled down the brim of his hat, and trudged off through the snow.

20

WOUNDED PRIDE

Finn wasn't expecting for it to snow. If he had known beforehand, he would have ridden another horse rather than the one towing the sledge. Even though the two ends of the poles glided better over the slick ground, the small hipparion horse was sometimes having trouble on the rough terrain and stumbling on rocks buried under the snow.

Reaching the base of an incline, Finn jumped off his horse. He motioned for Ash to do the same. They grabbed the ropes looped around the horses' necks and guided them up the rise onto the crest of a knoll. Down below, the hillside sloped to the flatlands, which was already blanketed in white.

But Finn wasn't discouraged. He knew where they could still find good grass.

Finn and Ash led their horses down to the outskirts of the forest bordering the winterized prairie. Tall, lush grass grew lavishly around the trunks, the vegetation shielded under the low hanging branches shrouded with snow.

The primitive men walked their horses under the canopy and hitched each animal to a separate tree. Working together, they removed a folded tarp from the travois on Finn's horse and spread it out on the ground. Finn began cutting down the grass with a machete while Ash gathered up the trimmings and laid them on the ground cloth. It didn't take them long before they had amassed a large mound of cuttings.

Finn and Ash lifted the tarp and carried it over to the sledge behind Finn's horse then strapped it down and covered the load to keep it dry for the trip back.

They were about to remove the folded canvas from the travois behind Ash's horse when Finn heard a noise back in the trees. He raised his hand, motioning for Ash to be quiet and listen.

Without saying a word, both men stared in the direction of the sound and moved backward toward their horses. Even though the machete in Finn's hand was a formidable weapon, he laid the blade down on the sledge and grabbed his spear. He looked over at Ash and saw that his friend had already notched an arrow in his bow.

Finn's keen senses could differentiate the fluttering wings from the branches rustling in the snowy breeze above his head, and when he inhaled deeply through his pug nose, he didn't have to see the animal to know what it was.

He looked over and knew Ash had identified the scent as well.

Holding his spear out in front in a battle stance, Finn watched as a sabertooth cat stepped out into the open. It was a young male with large paws, which meant it would be a big animal when it became an adult. Finn knew if he got down on his hands and knees, the cat would be taller than him at the shoulders and outweighed him considerably. He stared at the young cat's impressive set of white tusk-shaped fangs.

Finn couldn't help thinking what a fine pelt its spotted brown fur would make though he and the rest of the Paranthropus tribe had made a promise to Sterling and Tonya to protect the bio-engineered mammals the scientists had created and would only kill one if they found their lives to be in danger.

At the moment, the young male wasn't posing any imminent threat and was keeping its distance, pacing back and forth twenty feet away. Finn hoped it was just curious, having never seen them there before.

The horses began to snort and shake their manes. Finn's horse yanked back its head and snapped off the branch that it was tied to. The scared horse tried backing up but it was near impossible with the cumbersome sledge blocking its rump.

Finn saw something out of the corner of his eye.

When he spun around a full-grown female sabertooth bounded out of the trees and pounced onto the back of Ash's horse, buckling its legs as it was taken down.

Ash pulled back the bowstring and released his arrow. The projectile struck the big cat in the shoulder. Ignoring the pain, the predator sunk its fangs into the horse's neck but not before Ash unleashed another arrow, this time striking the big cat in the throat.

The mortally wounded sabertooth pawed the arrow and snapped off the shaft, which opened up the gash even more. Blood gushed down her chest and she collapsed onto the ground.

Seeing the dead horse on the ground only made Finn's horse even more frantic. It thrashed side to side until it broke free of the poles strapped over its shoulders. Turning to run, the horse only made it a few feet before another sabertooth cat appeared out of nowhere and latched onto the horse's hindquarters with its deadly claws. The big cat used the weight of its body to drag the horse down to the ground.

Finn threw the spear only to miss as it sailed over the sabertooth cat's head. He glanced around for the machete but didn't see it anywhere.

He heard a noise behind him and glanced over his shoulder.

His heart lumped in his throat when he saw six adult sabertooth cats staring back at him and what must be the rest of the pride. He turned to Ash who had set another arrow on his bow but hadn't bothered to pull back the bowstring when he realized there were too many for him to kill.

With nowhere to run and mere seconds away from being mauled and eaten alive, Finn pointed his finger at the sky and yelled, "Up, up, up!"

Finn dashed toward one tree, Ash another. They shimmied up the tree trunks at the same time like a couple of scampering primates, grabbing one limb after another, squeezing through the branches and dislodging clumps of snow, pulling themselves up like they were scaling rungs on a ladder.

A sabertooth cat sprang up the tree after Finn as another big cat clawed its way up the trunk after Ash. Shoving their big heads up through the branches, the giant cats were only able to climb up twenty feet before the limbs became too thick for them to fit through and they eventually had to find their way back down.

Finn made it almost to the top and sat on a limb. He saw Ash in the other tree and waved to his friend. He gazed down at the ground one hundred feet below.

The sabertooth cats were gathered in two groups, lying on their bellies near the base of the trees, eating the dead horses.

21

VENT HOLE

Grant was an excellent tracker when it came to hunting deer so when he grabbed his hunting rifle and snowshoes he thought it wouldn't be much of a challenge finding Christian, whom he assumed had hiked only a mile or so down the trail.

But then the heavy snowfall on the ground quickly made it near impossible to find any signs of which way the paleontologist might have gone, as there were no obvious footprints to follow.

The pathway was ten feet wide in places by the constant use of the dune buggies, which meant there was a slim chance to none of Christian having to squeeze through the brush and snag a piece of his clothing or maybe accidentally snap off a branch, leaving any telltale evidence that he had passed this way.

The snow was up to Grant's ankles so he stopped. He removed the snowshoes slung over his back and placed them on the ground. He slipped his right boot into the toe strap and got down on his left knee to tighten the binding. He fastened the heel strap and used the ratcheting mechanism to form it around the heel of his boot before cinching that strap. He did the same with his other foot and stood up.

Continuing down a gentle slope, Grant had to walk with his feet farther apart so as not to tread on the insteps of the snowshoes and wished he had thought to bring along his ski poles. The poles not only helped him keep his balance but the tips of the poles could be used to prod the snow-covered ground for any hidden tripping hazards such as buried logs and loose rocks that might cause his feet to slide out from under him.

He heard cascading water off in the distance and knew it was from one of the glacial fed creeks traversing down the mountainside. He stepped from the trail and cut through a section of trees.

A few minutes later he came to a giant spruce that had uprooted and toppled down. He saw partial footprints made mostly by cloven hooves.

He recognized the two different sized paw prints as those of Sasha and Digger's.

There were human tracks as well, which had to belong to Christian.

By the looks of it, Sasha and Digger had ventured off and left Christian to travel on his own.

Which didn't surprise Grant.

Even though Sasha spent much of her time with Grant, especially when he was outdoors doing chores such as chopping firewood or out on a hunt, the dire wolf loved her morning romps with her playmate, Digger. It wasn't unusual for them to be gone for hours at a time.

"Jesus," Grant said when he saw the dead feral pigs lying in crimson patches of snow like abandoned corpses strewn on a wintry battlefield. Some of the boars were rather large, maybe three hundred pounds. He pulled a glove off with his teeth and placed his bare hand on a boar's side. Grant could feel the fading warmth through his fingertips, which meant the animal hadn't been dead for very long.

Slipping his glove back on, he walked over to the gaping hole in the ground where the tree had uprooted. He looked down and saw tiny piglets, each killed by a single savage bite. Seeing as none of the animals had been eaten, Grant suspected the carnage was the result of a rampaging hell pig.

Grant retraced his steps and picked up Christian's tracks. The imprints were deep enough to follow but wouldn't be for long before the snow covered them in. He was tempted to fire his rifle to see if he could get a response but figured he'd call out Christian's name instead.

After a third attempt, Grant thought he heard a reply.

"Christian! Where the hell are you?"

The voice was muffled but Grant swore he heard the words *Down here*.

"Say that again!" Grant trudged in the direction of the voice and had gone maybe fifty yards when he spotted Sasha and Digger. They were staring down at the ground and clawing at the snow.

Grant rushed over, stopping a few feet away from Sasha and Digger when he saw the circular hole in the ground. "Move back before you both fall in," he said and shooed them away with his hand.

"Grant? Is that you?"

"It's me," Grant replied, peering down with his hands on his knees.

Christian was standing at the bottom of a fifteen-foot deep pit. He stared up as the snow fell on his face. "Thank God you found me."

"I think you should be thanking Sasha and Digger. Are you hurt?"

"I don't believe so. How in the world did this happen?"

"You fell down a vent hole. They're all over this mountain."

"Can you get me out?"

"Hold on." Grant slipped the rifle's gun strap over his shoulder. He looked around and saw a small tree lying in the snow. He figured it was tall enough and would do the trick. He went over, pulled out his serrated hunting knife and began sawing the branches so they were only sticking out six inches from the trunk. Once he was done, he dragged the trunk to the edge of the hole. "Watch your head while I lower this down. You can use it like a ladder to climb out."

"Will do," Christian yelled up.

Grant shoved the end of the tree trunk down into the hole.

"I guess next time I'll be more careful," Christian said as he climbed out.

"Not your fault. This mountain can be pretty treacherous in the winter."

"You saw the dead pigs?" Christian asked.

"I did. I take it that was the work of a hell pig?"

"Wretched thing almost got us."

"You're lucky." Grant glanced around but didn't see hide nor hair of Sasha and Digger. "Now where did they go?"

"Who knows," Christian said with a laugh. "They're quite the disappearing act."

22

MEGATHERIUM

Gale was beginning to regret her snap decision to go on horseback in search of her friends as her tailbone was already aching from bouncing up and down on the horse's ridged spine. Her legs felt like they were going to cramp from having to hug the animal's ribs with the inside of her knees. Even though she was an accomplished rider in the saddle when she was younger, she never cared much for riding bareback.

She felt like a novice compared to Jasmine and Luna. The primitive women were naturals and clung to their horses like they were glued to their backs despite the animals being wet from the falling snow.

Which is why they kept to the trees whenever possible, veering off the trail so as not to be out in the open.

But that presented another challenge having to navigate through deadfalls and rock formations in the deep snow that sometimes came up to the underbellies of the small horses, forcing Gale, Jasmine, and Luna to dismount whenever they came to impassable snowdrifts and had to guide the horses up and over and around the obstacles.

Even though Gale feared for Sterling, Tonya, and Morgan's safety, she was also beginning to worry that maybe her rescue effort might end in tragedy for her and her two female companions. She was already chilled to the bone despite wearing water-repellent clothing and boots designed for subfreezing conditions.

Gale didn't want to be the one to decide if they should turn back as she knew Jasmine and Luna wouldn't give up just because of the cold.

The animal-skin clad women had endured harsher weather having lived in a cavern grotto. Even though the Paranthropus tribe members were only five-feet tall and weighed just under a hundred pounds each, they were the strongest and bravest women Gale had ever known.

Treading waist deep in the snow after Jasmine's horse, Gale kept a firm grip on her horse's reins while Luna trailed behind.

They were approaching what looked like a massive snowdrift piled around some trees at the base of a snow-covered hillock.

Jasmine's horse reared back without warning, almost plowing into Gale. "Hey, what the heck?" Her horse reacted the same way and almost yanked Gale off her feet.

The snowdrift suddenly exploded thirty feet in the air like it had been blown up by a demolition charge as a giant creature stood on its hind legs.

"Oh my God," Gale gasped. She gazed up at the massive megatherium. The giant ground sloth stood almost twenty feet tall and had to weigh four tons. It was using its thick tail as a tripod to balance its huge body. As it raised its arms chest high, Gale couldn't take her eyes off of the four-foot long curved claws on it forelegs.

She wasn't overly concerned as the giant ground sloth was a herbivore with a docile disposition, and only rarely—Gale saw dried blood caked on the sloth's mouth and snout—were meat eaters.

Before Gale could yell out a warning, the giant ground sloth took a lumbering step toward them and let out a bellowing roar that sounded like an enormous build up of gas belching from a basement boiler.

Gale heard something whiz above her head.

She glanced over her shoulder and saw Luna poised with her longbow.

The arrow struck the sloth in the shoulder, but then it bounced off, deflected by a protective layer of bony deposits on the animal's skin.

Jasmine shot an arrow, and it too, ricocheted.

The giant ground sloth dropped on all fours and charged.

Jasmine tried to turn her horse around but the snow was too deep. Her eyes locked with Gale's just as the behemoth came crashing down on Jasmine and her horse.

23

HEADDRESSES

Sitting inside the Quonset hut next to Maya at the kitchenette table, Janelle was amazed the young woman had already finished plucking her goose whereas Janelle was only halfway done with hers. Janelle liked to think it was because she had been taking the time to pile the feathers neatly on the table while Maya let hers land all over the floor which looked like the inside of a hen house after being raided by a fox.

Janelle never liked to waste anything and always found ways to repurpose items whenever she could. She planned to use the feathers in a goose down vest.

Maya had a different idea. She jumped up from the table and crossed the room to where Little Rook and Kelly were playing.

At first glance, the ape-faced toddlers looked like they were bouncing a small rubber ball back and forth but then Kelly yelled, "Me win," and scooped up the knucklebones between them.

"Not fair," Little Rook protested and tried to grab the game pieces that had once been the anklebones of small animals.

"No fight," Maya scolded the children. "Come."

Kelly dropped the ball and the bone pieces on the floor as she and Little Rook sprang to their feet.

Maya went over to her bunk. She took a moment and rummaged through the single drawer on her nightstand that had once been a metal three-drawer file cabinet, the bottom stuffed with incidentals. She pulled out a large roll of ribbon and showed it to the children. "Maya make surprise."

Janelle had finished removing the feathers from her goose and had both birds on a large cutting block on the counter. She was in the process of cleaning out the geese and slopping their innards into the sink when Maya and the kids came over to the table. She stopped what she was doing and watched as Maya sat down and unstrung two long strips of ribbon onto the surface of the tabletop.

Little Rook and Kelly stood on their tiptoes and were just tall enough to see over the edge of the table. Maya selected the best looking feathers and began to loop and tie them to the ribbons. Once she had a dozen or so attached to each one, she tied the ends together.

Janelle saw the excited looks on Little Rook and Kelly's faces when Maya placed the headdresses on their heads.

"Go play," Maya said.

The toddlers giggled and ran to the back of the Quonset hut. Little Rook pushed open the door and Kelly followed him outside.

Janelle smiled at Maya. "You better see they don't wander off."

But before Maya could get up from the table, Little Rook and Kelly were back inside chasing after one another, throwing snowballs at each other.

"What in the world." Janelle wiped her hands with a dishtowel and marched through the Quonset hut. Maya was right behind.

When Janelle opened the back door and saw everything covered in snow, she was surprised to see how much had fallen without her knowing and in such a short time. She stepped out onto the deck and looked around.

The horses were no longer in the corral.

Where was everyone?

She walked over to the edge of the porch and saw a shape lying on the ground beneath the trestle tower.

"Oh my God! Max!"

PART THREE
NEW HAVEN

24

BEAR BONES

Harden knew it was going to be cold this time of year especially in the early mornings and throughout the night and had planned accordingly making sure they had plenty of food for the journey and packed enough warm clothes. What he hadn't figured on was tackling the rough terrain in the snow.

"How much longer from here, do you think?" Darren asked, trudging up the steep mountainside behind Harden. Whenever possible, they would grab hold of small saplings to pull themselves up so as not to slip back down because of their heavy backpacks.

"Depends on the weather. Why, getting tired?" Harden spotted a rock ledge sprinkled with snow about thirty feet up where they could sit for a while. "Want to take a short break?"

"Nah, I'm okay."

Harden glanced back over his shoulder. "You sure?" They'd been hiking nonstop the entire morning.

"Really. I'm okay."

"Well, I'd like to take five." Harden was far from being tired and suspected that even if Darren were exhausted he would be too proud to admit it. There was no point in pushing the teenager. It wasn't like taking a five-minute rest break to hydrate was going to make that much difference and throw them off any kind of schedule.

Climbing up onto the rock shelf, Harden was surprised to see a cave. The entrance looked high enough for Harden to walk into without having to stoop.

"Think there's anything in there?" Darren asked as he joined Harden.

"Maybe we should check before we get too comfortable." Harden dropped his pack on the ground. He rammed back the bolt on his hunting rifle and put a live round inside the chamber. He waited while Darren took off his pack and grabbed a flashlight from a side pouch.

"You want me to go first as I have the light?" Darren asked.

"No, you better let me. Just stay close and shine the light in front." Harden kept his rifle at the ready and stepped inside the cave.

Darren followed closely behind and stayed to Harden's left so he could shine the beam straight ahead. "Boy, this is really big."

"Shine the light up," Harden instructed.

The beam swept across a limestone-crusted ceiling fifteen feet above their heads.

"Could be a large cavern," Harden said. "Want to see how far back it goes?"

"Sure! Let's check it out!" Darren said.

Harden detected the excitement in Darren's voice, like a kid about to go on an adventure for the first time with his dad. Even though the initial reason Harden had agreed to take Darren was solely because the teenager had a better knowledge of what medicines they should be requesting, he had to admit he was enjoying their time bonding together.

"Do you hear that?" Darren asked as they proceeded down the passage.

"We must be in a wet cave," Harden said upon hearing water drizzling down the sides of the surrounding walls. "Watch your step, it might get slippery." He rested the barrel of his hunting rifle in the crook of his left arm and concentrated on the cavern floor ahead.

"Whoa, look at that!" Darren said, when the beam of light shined on a large skeleton near the back wall.

Harden swung his gun around and pointed it straight ahead. With each step, he saw more skeletal remains strewn at the end of the cave. "Looks like a bear's den."

Darren stopped and panned the light from left to right.

There had to be over a hundred or so carcasses, most of them picked clean to the bone, some with rotted flesh still attached.

"Let me see the flashlight," Harden said. Once Darren passed him the light, Harden got a closer look at the bone yard, which comprised mostly of big animals like deer and elk.

"What do you think, a Kodiak?" Darren asked.

Kodiak bears were the largest in the region, some standing ten feet tall and weighing upwards of twelve hundred pounds.

"This wasn't a Kodiak or a grizzly." Harden shined the light on a skeleton. "See that skull?"

"Yeah."

"*That's* a Kodiak."

"But that's crazy. What could be bigger than a Kodiak?"

"The first time I made this trip one of my men was killed by what I later learned was a short-faced bear."

"Never heard of it."

"That's because it's prehistoric and shouldn't even exist. The one I saw stood twelve feet tall and had to weigh two thousand pounds, and believe it or not was created by these folks at the weather station. Don't ask me how, but they did."

"Think this is the same one?"

"I don't know. Sure hope not. We shot the hell out of it back then so if it's still alive I'm sure it's pissed. We best get out of here."

They were maybe fifty feet inside the cave.

Harden turned, and when he saw the oblong of daylight at the entrance, something humongous stepped inside the cave and blocked out the sunshine.

"Shit," Harden cursed, "it's come back!"

25

UNWANTED ADVANCES

"The rain has let up but I'm sure it won't be long before we see some snow," Emily said, staring up at the gray sky between the trees from the cabin doorway.

"We better get these kids over to the latrine before it starts up again." Debra had all four of her children stand in front of her so she could button up their coats.

"Do I have to go?" Danny asked.

Emily turned to her son. "We're all going. Better now than have to walk there in the pouring rain."

"But—"

"No buts. Put on your jacket and hat."

The six-year-old did what he was told rather than protest. He was a good kid though there were times he could be ornery. Emily knew Danny missed his father and was having trouble adjusting to not having a male parental figure in his life.

"Everyone ready?" Debra asked her two boys and twin girls.

The children all nodded that they were.

"Good. Let's go."

Emily stepped outside and waited for Debra, her children, and Danny to come out before closing the cabin door. Debra took the lead and they proceeded through the trees single file like a couple of teachers escorting a small group of school children on a nature hike.

The outdoor latrine was a short walk. It was a crudely constructed outhouse made of heavy-duty 5/8-inch marine plywood with a pitched roof. Inside, a plastic toilet seat was mounted on a wooden box.

The last person to use the facility had left the door open to air out the enclosed space.

Even so, Emily could smell the ripe commingling stench of urine and feces down inside the crapper pit. "Who's first?"

"Why don't you and Danny," Debra offered. "We could be a while."

"Sure," Emily said. She looked at her son. "Danny?"

"Okay!" the boy huffed. He held his nose and stepped inside. Emily began to close the door when Danny yelled out, "Mom!"

"Oh, sorry," she answered, forgetting how claustrophobic it could be sitting in the dark trapped with the nauseating smell. She left the door partially open but not enough so anyone could see inside.

Danny wasn't in there for more than thirty seconds before he pushed open the door and burst out. "Something died in there!"

"I know it's bad but I doubt that," Emily told her boy.

Debra looked at Emily. "You don't think an animal fell down the pit?"

"Maybe you should stick your head down there and take a look," Emily grinned.

"Shut up. Hurry up before my kids pee their pants."

Emily covered her nose and mouth with a scarf and went inside. Danny had been right; it did smell like something had died inside the outhouse. She pulled down her trousers and sat down on the cold toilet seat. She looked between her legs and swore she saw something swimming around down there. She closed her eyes, peed, and was zipping up the front of her trousers when she stepped outside.

"That bad, eh?" Debra said. "Think we should line the floor with pine branches?"

"It couldn't hurt," Emily said, knowing the fragrant pine needles were often effective as a natural air freshener even though she doubted if a forest could mask that foul smell. "Want me to gather some up?"

"How about I get the children to do that once they're done taking turns going to the bathroom. Maybe Danny could stay behind and help?"

Emily looked at her son.

"Do I have to?"

"You could be in charge."

Danny's eyes brightened. "Okay."

"I'll go back and fix us something to eat while you're doing that," Emily said.

"We shouldn't be long," Debra replied, ushering one of the twins into the latrine.

Emily made her way through the woods. When she got back, she found the cabin door open. She could have sworn she had closed it when they left.

She took a step inside and looked about the large room with the bunks in the back where the children slept, the long table with benches on either side where they ate their meals. Nothing looked out of the ordinary.

Without a lock that could be engaged from the outside, Emily always worried someone might sneak in while they were gone and steal what little they had. But that had never happened, thanks to Jim Harden who had a strict policy about thievery in the camp and threatened to expel anyone caught violating the rules.

Emily heard a noise behind her and when she turned to see what it was, a figure stepped out from behind the door. A hard slap to the face rocked her back on her heels and she fell onto the floor.

She looked up and saw Orson Terrell with his shotgun. The creep had been trying to come onto her ever since her husband had died. She wanted nothing to do with him and had been avoiding him every chance she got hoping he would get the message.

Terrell stared down at her with a lascivious sneer.

"How many times do I have to tell you? Leave me alone!" Emily said, scooting backwards on the floor.

"You keep saying that but I know you want it," Terrell answered.

"No! Get out of here or I'll scream!"

"And who do you think is going to hear you? Certainly not Harden."

"What do you mean?"

"He's gone. There's no one here to help you. Looks like it's just you and me."

"Debra should be back any second with the children."

"I don't think so."

"Help!" Emily yelled. "Someone help me!"

Terrell laid his shotgun on the table.

He moved closer to Emily and straddled her legs. "When is the last time you had some?" He took off his jacket and tossed it on the end of the table, along with his gun belt with a holstered semi-automatic pistol.

Terrell unbuckled his belt and unzipped the fly on his pants. "Stop making such a fuss. It's not like you're a virgin. If I were you I'd get busy and take off them clothes, unless you want me to mess up that pretty face of yours."

"Go to hell!" Emily screamed.

"Have it your way, slut!"

Emily heard a loud gunshot.

A look of surprise came over Terrell's face as he lurched forward and slammed facedown on top of Emily. She pushed the man off of her and sat up.

Danny stood by the table, his arms straight out, his small hands holding up Terrell's heavy handgun out in front of him.

"Oh, God." Emily crawled over to her son. She gently took Terrell's pistol from the boy and placed it on the table. She put her arms around her trembling son and squeezed him tight. "It's okay, Danny. It's okay."

"He was going to hurt you," Danny sobbed. "I had to stop him."

"And you did. Thank you, my brave boy," Emily said, tears streaming down her cheeks as she smothered Danny's face with kisses.

"Jesus Christ, what the hell did you do?"

Emily looked up and saw Craig Hoskins standing in the cabin doorway with his M4 carbine, staring down at Terrell's body on the floor.

"Go away! Leave us alone!"

"You killed him?" Hoskins yelled. "You bitch!" He raised the snub barrel on his assault rifle and aimed the muzzle at Emily and Danny.

"Don't even think about it," a voice said from outside. "Lay your weapon down or I put one in the back of your head."

Hoskins bent at the knees and placed his gun on the ground.

"Now get lost."

"What about—"

"Go!"

Hoskins stepped away as Nelson and Cynthia rushed inside the cabin.

Cynthia knelt to examine Emily's bruised cheek. "Terrell did this?"

Nelson tapped Terrell in the ribs with the toe of his boot. "Lucky for him he's dead."

Emily couldn't agree more, wishing it had been her that shot and killed the vile man instead of Danny.

26

SMOKE SCREEN

Department of Justice Special Agent Kevin Higgins stood on the riverbank waiting for his four-man special operations team to exit the floatplane and come ashore.

Once they had assembled on the beach, the military-clad group did a last minute weapons check.

Higgins signaled to the pilot looking from the cockpit window. The aviator had been instructed to stay with the amphibious aircraft and await the team's return once the mission was complete. Higgins was afraid if the pilot accompanied them and ended up getting shot, or even worse killed, they would be stranded.

"Think there's a chance they heard the plane's engine?" one man asked Higgins.

"I don't think so. That's why I had the pilot touchdown up river so we could drift down."

Upon consulting with a map, a soldier looked around at the surrounding forest and glanced out at the bend in the river. "Judging by the terrain, I'd say we're maybe five clicks away from the New Haven encampment."

"That would be about right," Higgins replied. The military terminology 'click' was equivalent to one kilometer, which was roughly three-fifths of a mile.

The soldier tucked the map away in the front pocket of his combat vest. "You really think Pierce is that vindictive he would come back here and massacre these people?"

"I hate to say it," Higgins said, "but the man's deranged."

"But there's no intel suggesting he's even here."

"Don't be so sure. Either way, our orders are to transport the women and children to a safe location."

"What about the men, they're criminals. Surely they'll put up a fight."

"Not when they hear Pierce might be coming to wipe out the entire camp," Higgins said. "I doubt they've forgotten how he ambushed them the last time he was here."

"But weren't you in charge of that mission?" the soldier asked.

"I was," Higgins replied. "But I never authorized the senseless killing. I'm hoping I can convince Jim Harden who runs the camp that we're here on good faith."

"You really think he's going to trust us?"

"It's worth a shot." Higgins looked at the other men. "Let's move out."

A soldier took the lead as forward observer while Higgins and the other men followed single file.

The plan was to cut through the thick forest for about two clicks until they reached the main trail then sneak up to the perimeter of the camp and assess the opposition before making their presence known.

But the plan quickly fell apart when they reached the path and saw Pierce standing in the middle of the trail like he was expecting them.

"Took you long enough," Pierce said in a sarcastic tone. He could have passed for a hunter in his camouflage jacket and trousers if he had been carrying a rifle, which he wasn't.

"Hold up," Higgins told his men. Two soldiers positioned themselves on either side of Higgins with their weapons trained on Pierce while the third man watched their rear.

"Should restrain him?" the forward observer asked as he pulled the coiled zip ties off his belt.

Higgins looked at Pierce who was standing twenty feet away. "Get on your knees, Pierce. I'm putting you under arrest."

"I don't think so," Pierce said and slowly opened the front of his jacket.

"Ah, shit," Higgins cursed when he saw Pierce wearing a grenadier's vest, the twenty-four pouches designed to hold projectile grenades that fit on the end of a grenade launcher. Some of the explosives on Pierce's vest were hand grenades.

Pierce held up a hand grenade for everyone to see. It was missing the pin. The only thing preventing it from exploding was his thumb pressing down on the striker spring. "I guess I don't have to tell you what happens when I let go."

"You don't strike me as a suicide bomber," Higgins said, calling Pierce's bluff.

Higgins knew a single grenade had a lethal range of sixteen feet and could still maim a person thirty feet away. He hated to think what twenty-four grenades would do; if there would be anything left of them after the destructive power of the concussion blew off their arms and legs and the shrapnel shredded their bodies into an unrecognizable hail of bloody pieces.

"Don't I?" Pierce said defiantly.

Higgins glanced at his men. He saw the indecision and fear in their eyes.

"What do you want to do, sir?" said the soldier to his left. "Do we take him down?"

Before Higgins could answer, two canisters lobbed out of the trees and landed directly at their feet, engulfing them in a thick cloud of smoke. A split second later a heavy barrage of machinegun fire ambushed them.

27

FAST EXIT

Nelson stood by while two of the camp's men carried Terrell's body out of the cabin. The man didn't deserve a proper burial, so Nelson told them to bury him somewhere out in the woods, as far away as possible.

"Thank you," Emily said, sitting at the table with Danny and Cynthia.

"The man was a pig. He deserved to die," Nelson said, and then regretted his words when he saw the pained expression on the boy's face.

"You should really let me examine your face," Cynthia said to Emily. "He may have fractured your cheekbone."

"No, it's okay. It's sore but I think it's fine," Emily replied with a sheepish grin.

Debra stepped in the doorway. "Is it okay if I bring the children inside?"

"Can you give us a minute," Cynthia said. "There's a little clean up that needs to be done first."

Debra walked over to her four children who were playing their version of a no rules soccer match, kicking a pinecone back and forth in the dirt.

Grabbing an old towel lying on the table, Cynthia asked Emily, "Do you mind if I use this? I can get you another one."

"Sure, go ahead."

Cynthia got down on her hands and knees and began mopping up the small pool of blood on the floor left by Terrell. She did the best job she could, bunched up the towel so no blood would drip out, and stood up.

Everyone reacted to the sound of distant gunfire.

"What was that?" Cynthia said.

Nelson stepped outside. "That was heavy machinegun fire. Sounded like it came from the direction of the river."

"Could it be Mason's men?" Cynthia asked.

"Not with that much fire power," Nelson said.

"Who do you think it is?" Emily asked.

"I don't know."

"You don't think it's them?" Cynthia prayed it wasn't the same government agents that had attacked them before.

"If it is, we need to leave now!"

Emily sprang from the table and rushed to the door. "Debra! We need to get the children out of here."

"What about our things?"

"Leave them. Everyone that way," Nelson said, pointing to the trees on the other side of the camp.

"Danny, let's go." Emily grabbed her son's hand and they ran after Debra and the children who were already halfway to the trees.

Nelson cupped his hands around his mouth and yelled, "Everybody, get out here!"

Half a dozen men with guns came out of their cabins, including Hoskins. "What the hell's going on?" Hoskins said.

"We're about to be raided! No time for questions. Stay with the women and children and head to Mason's place."

Hoskins glared obstinately at Nelson. "We don't take orders from you."

More gunshots could be heard in the distance, only this time they were closer.

"You heard Nelson," one man shouted, starting to jog away. "Let's get out of here." The other men dashed after him, leaving Hoskins standing alone. He hesitated only for a moment before running after the others.

"We can't just leave," Cynthia said. "What about the medical supplies?"

Nelson went back inside the cabin. He grabbed Terrell's shotgun off the table, and when he came back out he handed the handgun to Cynthia. "Won't be much good to us if we're all dead."

28

RAZED

A large group of men wearing camouflage battle fatigues and armed with M4 Carbine Commando machineguns with M203 grenade launchers, stepped out of the trees through the lingering smoke swirling around the bodies lying in the middle of the trail.

Bruno Pierce put the safety pin back in the hand grenade and stuffed the explosive device back in its pouch. A man went over to Pierce and handed him a machinegun in exchange for the grenadier's vest while the other men assembled at the edge of the trail, awaiting further orders. One of them stepped over to a soldier lying on the ground. He was about to fire a round into the soldier's skull when Pierce said, "Save your ammo, you're going to need it."

Waving his men forward, they proceeded down the trail. They hadn't gone far when they spotted two men in the trees with their backs turned, digging what looked like a grave as there was a corpse lying next to a mound of dug up dirt.

Pierce signaled to one of his men, who snuck up behind the two unsuspecting gravediggers and shot them both in the back. Their shovels slipped from their hands as they toppled headfirst into the shallow pit.

"How much further to the camp?" a man asked.

"We're almost there," Pierce replied. "Remember what I told you."

"No prisoners, we got it."

They crept through the trees until they reached the outskirts of the encampment, which looked abandoned.

"Where is everyone?" one man asked.

"The cowards must have heard our gunshots and run off into the woods to hide," another man laughed.

"Quit gloating and get to work," Pierce said.

The men split up and dispersed about the camp. Two men marched over to the first cabin, kicked in the door, and strafed the interior with a quick burst of machinegun fire. A man stepped inside, and after a moment came back out. "All clear."

The man wearing the grenadier's vest tossed a grenade into the cabin and yelled, "Fire in the hole," as he ran for cover. A plume of black smoke belched out the front door with a loud boom as the cabin's walls shattered and the roof collapsed in on itself.

"One down, nine to go," Pierce said, standing at a safe distance while his men went from one cabin to the other razing the structures to the ground.

Soon there was nothing left of New Haven but smoldering rubble.

A grin crept over Pierce's face as he surveyed the destruction and the rising smoke billowing into the trees. "Let's go find them and finish the job."

29

LEFT FOR DEAD

Higgins' chest and back ached all over like a mad man had taken pleasure battering him with a ball peen hammer. When he took a deep breath, the expanding air in his lungs only exacerbated the pain. His right thigh burned where a bullet had grazed him and his left arm throbbed like a son of a bitch.

When he opened his eyes he saw blood oozing from the entry and exit holes in his coat sleeve from the through-and-through.

He sat up and looked at his team lying motionless on the ground. He could tell by their extensive wounds and the vast pools of blood they were all dead. He stared down at the crimson patch in the dirt where he had been lying, thankful to be alive.

Higgins unzipped his jacket with his right hand and grabbed the Velcro straps on his bulletproof vest. The straps made a ripping sound when he yanked them from their adhesive strips. As soon as he loosened the body armor he could breathe easier. He felt around the front of the vest with his fingers and discovered five bullets dimpled in the ballistic resistant polymer. He figured there were more slugs lodged in the back portion.

He opened his shirt and saw the bruising welts on his chest. Shrugging out of his jacket, he unsnapped the emergency first aid bag from his belt. After disinfecting and bandaging his arm, he unbuckled his belt, lowered his trousers, and stuck an adhesive patch over the cut on his thigh.

Once he was through doctoring himself, he redressed, tightened his bulletproof vest and zipped up his jacket.

He got to his feet, and just to be thorough, he went around to check each man for a pulse even though he knew it would be a waste of time. He glanced at his watch and realized he'd been unconscious for almost an hour, which meant Pierce was most likely already at the camp.

Higgins tried to remember the moment they were ambushed but it was all a blur.

He had no idea what he was up against. For all he knew Pierce could have five, ten, maybe upwards of twenty mercenaries with him.

Was he willing to go up against such overwhelming odds single-handedly?

He had two choices. He could go back to the floatplane and abort the mission.

Or he could go after Pierce and God knows how many of his followers.

Higgins heard an explosion off in the distance. Less than a minute later, he heard another one followed by several more. He saw dark smoke drifting up into the sky.

"Screw it," he said and began collecting a cache of guns and ammunition for the fight of his life, praying it didn't turn out to be a foolhardy suicide mission.

30

HEAVY MEAL

Hidden under a smelly heap of bones, Harden peeked out at the short-faced bear only ten feet away as it used its gigantic claws to savagely disembowel and rake the hide off the large elk the monstrous predator had dragged into its den.

Before every bite, the humongous bear would let out a forceful snort and make a rumbling sound in the back of its throat, the loud sounds reverberating off the interior walls of the cavern like a chugging locomotive paused midway in a tunnel.

"Think it can smell us?" Darren whispered, lying beside Harden.

"Not with all that blood lathered on its face," Harden replied in a hushed voice.

The massive bear reminded Harden of a big kid sitting in the middle of his room surrounded by his favorite toys.

Only the accumulated carcasses weren't playthings.

Even though Harden had his hunting rifle, he doubted if it would be enough to take down the gigantic beast. Sitting on its rump, the bear's head was almost touching the ceiling. It tore a leg section off of the dead elk and lifted it up to its gaping mouth, ripping flesh with its sharp teeth and snapping bone in its powerful jaws.

Repositioning itself to get comfortable, the behemoth scooted backward, crushing large skeletons under its massive weight and stopping a foot short from sitting on top of both of them.

Harden looked over at Darren.

The young man had his head down on his forearms and his eyes closed like an ostrich hiding its head in the sand, figuring he would be better off not seeing what could be his imminent death.

Darren opened his eyes when Harden gave him a gentle nudge with his elbow.

They lay motionless for the next thirty minutes. That's how long it took for the short-faced bear to finish its heavy meal and lie down on its belly. It didn't take more than a couple of minutes until the slumbering beast was snoring.

Judging by all the dead animals stockpiled in the cave, Harden wondered if the bear had been gorging itself in preparation for a dormant hibernation.

Just to be safe, they waited a while longer before making their first move. It was tricky crawling out from under the bones without making much noise.

When Darren was beginning to stand, he stepped on a piece of bone. Even though it hardly made a sound, to Harden and Darren it was like the loud crack of a gunshot.

The bear shifted slightly and continued to snore.

Harden and Darren carefully crept through the cave and stepped outside.

Their backpacks were where they had left them covered in snow and had not been disturbed. Quietly, they grabbed their gear and began to trudge up the mountainside.

Once they were a fair distance away from the cave, Harden stopped and looked at Darren. "You okay? That was pretty scary back there."

"To be honest I really thought we were done for," Darren admitted.

"We were lucky, that's for sure. Made it out of there by the skin of our teeth."

"Yeah, just barely."

Harden let out a boisterous laugh and clapped Darren on the back. "Scared or not, it's nice to see you haven't lost your sense of humor."

PART FOUR
NORTH STAR
WEATHER STATION

31

HUNG OUT TO DRY

Wearing only a foil emergency blanket and her waterproof boots, Tonya stomped her feet to stay warm in front of the campfire that she and Sterling had made as it continued to snow.

Morgan had strung a clothesline under the branches between two trees so the heat of the fire could dry their wet garments, which were still a little damp and were beginning to stiffen from the freezing temperature.

Tonya felt her shirt. It was like a frozen packet of meat that had been partially thawed out in the microwave oven. She had to peel the fabric apart as it was sticking together to make it pliable enough to put on. She removed her pants, underwear briefs, sports bra and socks from the line.

Sterling and Morgan, also draped in the emergency blankets, were too busy working on the dune buggy they had managed to get back on its tires to notice her shrug out of the heat-retaining foil.

Standing naked under the falling snow, she kicked off her boots so she could slip on her briefs and then step into her pants. She fastened her bra and put on her shirt. She went over and sat on a rock to slip on her socks and boots. Once she was done, Tonya grabbed her parka off the clothesline. The lining was damp in places but it was too cold to wait for it to dry properly. She put on her coat, zipped it up and yelled out to the men, "I think your clothes are ready!"

"We're almost done," Morgan called out. He got behind the steering wheel of the dune buggy and turned the starter key.

The electric motor responded with a glorious hum.

Sterling jumped into the front passenger seat and they drove over to Tonya who was standing by the campfire, rubbing her hands together.

"Am I a genius or what?" Morgan said, turning off the motor and climbing out of the vehicle.

"If you say so," Tonya said. "At least now we won't have to hike back."

Sterling got out on his side and walked over to the clothes hanging on the rope strung between the trees. "They feel dry enough."

"The faster you two get dressed," Tonya said, "the faster we can get out of here."

"Enjoy the show," Morgan said.

"That's my line," Sterling told his friend.

Tonya turned her back. "Just hurry up."

"We can use the emergency blankets as tarps to put over the roll bar and shield us from the snow," Morgan said, as he started putting on his clothes.

"Good idea," Sterling said.

Once Sterling and Morgan were dressed, Tonya dumped handfuls of snow on the campfire to put it out while the men rigged the emergency blankets on the dune buggy.

They climbed aboard: Morgan at the wheel, Sterling in the seat next to him, Tonya sitting in the back.

Morgan turned the key, and when nothing happened, he went, "Uh-oh."

"You can't be serious," Tonya groaned.

Morgan and Sterling looked back over their shoulders at Tonya. At first their faces were serious and then they both burst out laughing.

"Just kidding," Morgan said and started the vehicle for real.

"I swear, one of these days, Morgan." But Tonya was laughing too hard to be angry, thankful that they were finally on their way home as they plowed through the snow along the shoreline of the lake.

32

TREED

Finn woke with a start when he heard something smash into the tree trunk just above his head and pine needles rained down on him. He brushed them out of his hair. He realized while he had been sleeping it must have snowed as everything around him was more white than green.

From his high perch, he could see the snowy tundra stretching for miles beyond the edge of the forest.

The dome of the sun was sinking behind the distant snowcapped mountain range.

Soon it would be nightfall.

An object flew at him and almost hit him in the face. At first he thought it was a bird but when he gazed down, he saw a pinecone careening down through the branches.

Finn gazed over at the next tree and saw Ash standing on a branch with another pinecone in his throwing hand. The ape-faced man had a big grin on his face. "Finn, wake up! No sleep!"

Finn shook his fist and shouted, "Ash in big trouble!" He looked for something to throw back but there were no pinecones within reach. He crouched on a bough and peered down through the tree limbs. The ground surrounding the base of the tree was covered in parts by fresh snow but mostly stained with large patches of blood and gore.

The sabertooth cats had eaten most of the horses, leaving the heads and the stripped away hides and bones to be picked over by the nighttime scavengers that would soon be prowling once it was dark.

He moved about the high branches with the grace of a gymnast and kept looking down but didn't see any sign of the big cats. He looked over at Ash. "Do you see?"

Ash shook his head.

"We go down!" Finn fearlessly dropped through the branches, controlling his fast descent by grabbing tree limbs and quickly releasing them as he swung down to the next branch all the way down for eighty feet. He stopped when he had almost reached the bottom and looked around to make sure there were no sabertooths waiting to pounce on him the second his feet touched the ground.

He dropped down and landed in the snow. He stayed in a crouch and turned his head both ways expecting to be attacked but he wasn't. Relieved, he stood and walked over to the next tree. He looked up and said, "You come down!"

Ash made his way down the tree and jumped down next to Finn. "What we do now?" Ash asked.

"Horses dead. We go home," Finn replied.

They traipsed through the snow in search of anything they might be able to take back with them. Each travois was a total loss. The poles were no longer attached and the tarps were ripped and were no use to them.

Finn dug around in the snow but couldn't find his spear. He looked around but didn't see any sign of the dead sabertooth, Ash had killed.

Ash located his longbow, but after an extensive search, he wasn't able to scrounge up a single arrow.

Without any true weapons except the knives on their sashes, the two Paranthropus tribesmen set out on the arduous hike back to the outpost.

33

EXCAVATORS

Gale had watched in horror as the giant ground sloth toppled down on top of Jasmine and her horse. She wasn't sure if the clumsy behemoth had stumbled as it was forced to walk on the sides of its feet because of its extremely long curled claws, or if it had purposely fallen on her friend.

Either way, there was little hope Jasmine had escaped from being crushed under the eight thousand pound creature.

Spooked by the humongous sloth, Gale's horse pulled from her and tried to run away but the snow was too deep for it to get very far.

Luna fired an arrow at the sloth's head. The arrowhead sank deep into the soft tissue above its right eye. The animal reacted from the sudden pain and reared back on its haunches to swipe at its face.

Gale waved her arms in the air to get the sloth's attention while Luna made her way through the waist-deep snow to outflank the animal. Making sure to stay clear of its powerful tail, Luna climbed up the thick-skinned animal's spine to the back of its shoulders. She took one of her arrows and stabbed the sloth repeatedly in the back of the neck.

The giant ground sloth turned so quickly to see what was inflicting the pain, Luna was sent flying and landed flat on her back in the snow.

Gale feared Luna was about to feel the wrath of the angry beast, but instead, the giant ground sloth decided to lick its wounds and go on its merry way and lumbered off, leaving a huge impression in the snow.

"We have to find Jasmine!" Gale screamed. She rushed over and began digging in the snow with her gloved hands. Luna bent down and began to dig like a dog, throwing clumps of snow out between her legs. They quickly unburied the horse's head. Its eyes were open but it was obvious by the blank stare the animal was dead.

Frantically, they kept digging.

"Gale! Luna find!" Luna shouted. Gale hurried over and helped to pull Jasmine out of the snow. The diminutive woman was unconscious and wasn't breathing.

Gale put her mouth to Jasmine's mouth and began blowing puffs of air. Jasmine's chest rose slightly. Gale performed some chest compressions and was about to go back to mouth-to-mouth when Jasmine came around and opened her eyes.

"Thank God," Gale said.

Jasmine sat up. The three of them hugged with joy. It was also a good way to warm Jasmine up as she was shivering from being compressed under the snow.

"I think we should go back," Gale said. She expected the two women to go along with her decision, but instead they shook their heads.

"Find Finn," Jasmine said, adamantly.

"And Ash,' Luna piped in.

"But we've lost a horse," Gale said.

"No care. Jasmine walk."

"How about we do this," Gale said, hoping they would listen to reason. "You and Luna can ride together and I'll take the other horse. We can keep looking but if we don't find them in an hour or so, we'll have to head back. I don't think we want to be out here after dark. Grant and the others can help us search tomorrow. What do you say?"

Jasmine and Luna exchanged looks and nodded.

"Good," Gale said. "Let's get the horses."

* * *

An hour later, Gale, Jasmine, and Luna came across the gory remains of Finn and Ash's dead horses at the edge of the forest. The Paranthropus women's first reaction was to search to see if their mates were buried under the snow.

Gale's heart sank when she saw all the blood surrounding the carnage and the large paw prints.

Jasmine was the one to find Finn's spear. She dropped to her knees and let out a bloodcurdling scream. Luna began to wail.

It was at that moment Gale knew they were too late and both men were dead.

34

MOVING THE BIG MAN

Janelle called out to Maya to come help her. Max was unconscious from his fall and was too big for Janelle to lift by herself. She knelt next to her husband and tried to get him to respond as the snow came down in a steady flurry.

"Max, wake up! Don't do this to me again," she said, remembering how she thought he was dead a time back after he fell off the modular when he was installing a section of roof and ended up shooting himself with the nail gun.

He let out a groan but didn't open his eyes.

She wasn't sure of the extent of his injuries but at least the big lug was alive.

Maya ran out of the Quonset hut's back door and down the porch steps.

Little Rook and Kelly came out to see what was going on and were still wearing the headdresses Maya had made for them.

"We need to get Max inside," Janelle explained to Maya.

They got on each side of Max and tried to lift him off the ground but weren't able to budge him as he was too heavy.

"We have to figure out another way." Janelle got to her feet and ran over to the shed between the Quonset hut and the Meads' modular home.

Opening the shed door, she spotted the ropes and pulleys inside that Gale had said she once used to pull heavy crates fastened to a sled up the nearby hillside. Janelle waved Maya over. She pointed to the gear Maya needed to bring outside.

Janelle used her ingenuity and jury-rigged a pulley system between the trestle tower and the top of the Quonset hut's doorway. She used some straps and a couple of six-foot long planks which they were able to roll Max onto. She cinched the straps and hooked them to a rubber grommet on the long rope stretching to the backdoor.

"Okay, heave!" Janelle said. Together, she and Maya pulled on the rope and lifted Max off the ground. Janelle repeated the command each time and with each pull, Max moved closer to the doorway.

Little Rook and Kelly were excited and ran down the steps. They got behind Maya and grabbed the rope to help.

Janelle shouted, "Heave," and could hear the little ones grunt. She doubted if their efforts made any difference but it was gratifying to see the children pitching in.

Once Max was level with the deck, Janelle anchored the rope to a low beam on the trestle tower. She went up the steps with Maya so they could push Max across the deck.

Janelle ducked inside and came out with two swivel chairs on casters. She positioned the chairs facing inward so that when they lowered Max strapped to the boards, his head was resting on one chair, his feet on the other.

They wheeled Max into the Quonset hut to the closest bunk.

"Okay, let's roll him into bed." Janelle lifted one end of the planks while Maya scooted out the chair so they could slide Max's upper body onto the bunk. They did the same with his feet and laid him flat on the mattress.

Janelle sat on the edge of the bunk and patted her husband's bearded face. "Max, can you hear me? Max, wake up!"

Max slowly opened his eyes and looked up at Janelle. "Whoa, what happened?"

"You took a fall. Are you hurt anywhere?"

"I don't think so."

"Does your head hurt?"

"A little."

"Try wiggling your fingers."

Max raised both hands and moved his fingers.

"How about your feet?"

"Yeah, I can feel my toes in my boots."

"I swear," Janelle said, "one of these days you're going to take a header and—"

"Hey, are you crying?" Max said.

"Shut up and lie still before I wallop you."

35

SNOW SQUALL

The weather continued to take a drastic turn for the worst. The strong gusty winds had turned the snow flurries into sharp icy pellets, making the hike up the mountain extremely challenging, especially as Grant was the only one wearing snowshoes.

In order for Christian to keep up and avoid sinking in the snow, he had to follow closely behind Grant so he could step into his impressions.

Grant felt Christian's hand on his shoulder.

"You sure this is the way?" Christian shouted, hunched over and holding onto his hat with one hand so it didn't blow off his head.

"Yeah, pretty sure," Grant yelled over his shoulder. Even though Grant had hiked up and down most of the mountainside, he was not familiar with this part of the forest. In all honesty he couldn't swear they were taking a direct route back to the outpost.

He was beginning to wish Christian hadn't ventured so far off the beaten path, and couldn't help feeling a little annoyed with the man when the paleontologist hollered into Grant's ear, "I can't feel my face!"

"Well, join the crowd!" Grant snapped. His legs were tired from walking in the cumbersome snowshoes and he wanted to stop and rest but it was out of the question. If they didn't keep moving, they would freeze to death.

Christian grabbed Grant's shoulder again. "Oh my God! What's that?"

Squinting his eyes, Grant gazed up ahead.

Two four-legged shapes stood further up the snowy hillside.

Grant grabbed the gun strap ever so slowly and removed the hunting rifle from his shoulder. He lifted the barrel and tucked the stock into his shoulder.

He peered through the high-power scope. "Oh my God is right."

"What are they?"

"Who do you think they are?" Grant lowered his rifle and yelled up, "Get your butts down here, right now!"

Sasha and Digger bounded down the slope.

36

WHITEOUT

Gale tried consoling Jasmine and Luna but they were too distraught, bawling their eyes out over Finn and Ash like two grief-stricken widows at a funeral.

"So you found Finn's spear. So what?" Gale said. "They could still be alive."

Jasmine stopped crying and hiccupped. "Finn not dead?"

There was no way for Gale to know for certain. She hated to lie but she didn't see any other way to persuade them and said, "I'll bet anything he's already at the weather station, probably waiting for us to show up."

"Ash, too?" Luna asked, still sniveling.

"I'm sure Ash is there as well. We need to get going. It'll be dark soon."

"Gale right. We go." Jasmine was still holding Finn's spear when she stood. She stepped over to her horse, and stabbed the spearhead into the snow. She grabbed the horse's mane, and like an accomplished stunt rider, swung onto the animal's back.

Luna ran over and vaulted onto the horse's rump right behind Jasmine as the woman snatched up the spear.

Gale mounted her horse with less bravado.

They rode into the forest and headed up an incline that looked like it might be the trailway leading to the weather station.

The higher up they went, the heavier the snowfall seemed to be coming down.

Icy pellets stung Gale's face as she didn't want to let Jasmine and Luna out of her sight.

As dusk approached, they found themselves riding into a whiteout of sleet, forcing the women to lay prone across the backs of their horses.

Gale clung onto her horse's mane and gave the animal free rein, hoping that it knew the way back even though she was skeptical if it had been domesticated enough to be barn spoiled.

She fought to stay awake, afraid if she fell asleep she would fall off her horse and freeze to death in the snow. She was chilled to the bone. Her face burned from the cold and tiny icicles had formed on her eyelashes. Her lungs were gelid from the frigid air.

Her eyes were irritated like they had sand in them so she closed her eyelids and rubbed them figuring her corneas were inflamed from not wearing sunglasses.

When she opened her eyes, the white landscape was glaring and hurt her eyes even more. She rubbed them again.

But when Gale reopened her eyes, she saw nothing.

She was suffering from a bad case of photokeratitis...Snow blindness.

37

STANDUP COMIC

The dune buggy labored up the snow bank. Morgan kept the accelerator pedal pegged to the floor to get maximum power but knew he was only draining the battery.

Even the balloon tires, which could navigate over just about any type of rough terrain, were getting bogged down in the deep snow.

"There goes the last emergency blanket," Tonya hollered from the back seat as the strong wind ripped the foil they were using as a canopy off the top of the roll bar.

"Watch out!" Sterling shouted.

Morgan cut the wheel and narrowly missed crashing into the side of a boulder that was barely visible under a snowdrift looming on the right side of the wide track they were following through the trees.

Tonya looked down at her feet and saw smoke billowing out from the bottom of Morgan's seat. "Pull over!" she screamed. "The buggy's on fire!"

Morgan only had to lift his foot off the accelerator for the UTV to come to a stop.

"Everyone out!" Sterling shouted and jumped out. Tonya vaulted from the back seat. Morgan grabbed the shotgun mounted between the front bucket seats before leaping from the vehicle.

They watched Morgan's seat catch fire. The plastic upholstery smelled god awful as it began to melt and the caustic flames quickly engulfed the rest of the dune buggy, creating a thick plume of black smoke. Snowflakes swirled around the rising smoke giving the illusion of a stationary tornado.

"Better not stand too close in case the battery explodes," Sterling said, pulling Tonya further away even though it was tempting to stand in front of the burning vehicle to stay warm despite the toxic fumes and the acrid smoke.

Morgan waved for Sterling and Tonya to follow him up the snow bank. "Come on. We're almost there."

After a few minutes hiking up the mountain, Morgan said, "Don't you think it's a little ironic?"

"What's that?" Sterling asked.

"We're living in a weather station and we had no idea this storm was coming."

"Well, it's not like we're meteorologists."

"Even if we were," Tonya piped in, "we would be allowed a fifty-fifty margin of error. When have you ever known a weatherman to get it right every time?"

"I would make a great weatherman," Morgan said. "I can tell you exactly what to expect for tonight. You know what my prediction is?"

"No, what?" Sterling asked.

"It doesn't take a genius to know the forecast for tonight will be *dark*."

"Very funny," Sterling said, "forgive me if I forget to laugh. Shame you never thought to take your standup routine on the road."

"What do you think I'm doing?" Morgan replied.

Sterling looked up and saw the silhouette of the Quonset hut in the raging snowstorm. "We made it!"

They climbed the steep slope and trudged through the snow to the porch steps in the blinding wind. All of the patio furniture had been blown off the deck and was scattered out on the snow.

Crossing the deck, Morgan managed to push the door open, letting in a flurry of snow. He held the door open for Tonya and Sterling as they entered the Quonset hut.

Morgan stepped inside and shoved the door shut.

"Thank God you're back," Janelle said, standing in the center of the oblong room.

Sterling saw Max lying on one of the bunks. "Is he okay?"

"He took a nasty fall. But yes, he's fine."

Maya rushed over and gave Tonya a great big hug. "Maya missed Tonya."

"I missed you, too," Tonya replied, returning the embrace.

Little Rook and Kelly scampered over and clung onto Sterling's legs. "Hey, kiddies," Sterling said, overjoyed by the fond reception.

Tonya looked around. "I don't see Grant or Christian. Haven't they come back yet?"

"No," Janelle said. "Neither have Sasha or Digger."

"What about Gale?"

"She left with Jasmine and Luna to go look for Finn and Ash."

"You mean they're still out there?" Tonya said.

"I'm afraid so," Janelle replied.

"Shouldn't we go look for them?" Sterling asked Morgan.

"We can't go out there in this. We'll have to wait until the weather clears up."

Everyone jumped when the howling wind slammed the metal side of the Quonset hut like a giant fist.

Sterling looked at his friend. "Judging by the sound of that, this storm isn't letting up anytime soon."

38

BLIZZARD

Gale called out to Jasmine and Luna but didn't know if they could hear her with the wind yowling through the trees. Being blind in the freezing cold only exasperated her situation as she tried not to panic.

She prayed her horse was conditioned to follow Jasmine's horse and hadn't wandered off aimlessly getting them lost. She couldn't feel her fingers and quickly realized she was no longer clinging to the horse's mane when she lost her balance and slid off the horse.

Landing facedown in the snow, Gale could hear her horse continue on without her. She raised her head and shouted, "Hey, come back here!" but she might as well have been yelling at the moon for what good it did her. She wiped the wet snow from her face and rolled onto her back.

Gale was exhausted and knew once she fell asleep it wouldn't be long before her body shutdown. She missed Grant and their beautiful life together. She knew she would never see him again. The thought of him finding her badly decomposed body after the first thaw made her want to cry but the freezing cold wouldn't allow the moisture to leak out of her tear ducts.

"Damn it!" she cursed.

Even though she couldn't see, she sensed a presence.

"Is someone there?" She could feel hot breath on her face.

"Sasha move!" a stern voice said.

"Grant? Is that you? I've gone snow-blind."

"Yes, it's me. My God, Gale, what are you even doing out here?"

"We were looking for Finn and Ash."

"And did you find them?"

Gale shook her head. "Are Jasmine and Luna all right?"

"They went with Christian and Digger. Here, wrap your arm around my neck and I'll carry you."

Gale felt his strong arms lift her off the ground.

She pressed her face into his collar.

"Don't ever scare me like that," Grant said, but she could tell he wasn't mad.

* * *

Morgan and Sterling were waiting by the back door when Grant came up the porch steps with Gale in his arms.

"Here, let me help you," Max said, nudging Sterling and Morgan out of the way. The big man took Gale, carried her over to a cot, and laid her down.

"Looks like you're back to your old self," Sterling commented.

"Hard to keep a good man down," Janelle said with a smile.

"We need to get her out of those wet clothes," Tonya said, and began undressing Gale. Janelle draped a blanket over the shivering woman.

"Someone needs to get under the covers with her and generate some heat."

Jasmine crawled under the blanket. Luna slid in as well.

Little Rook and Kelly climbed up on the cot.

"No, not you," Maya said, pulling the toddlers onto the floor. She shooed them into the kitchenette where Sasha and Digger were lying on the floor next to their water dishes.

Soon Gale stopped shaking and Jasmine and Luna got off the cot. The two women stepped away and went over to the other side of the room.

Janelle brought over a hot cup of tea.

"Thanks," Gale said, taking the mug as she sat up. She felt strange being the center of attention, sensing everyone was staring at her like she was some oddity at a state fair.

Tonya picked up on it right away and said, "Maybe we should let Gale rest."

"Good idea," Sterling agreed.

Christian walked over to a desktop covered with a small assortment of animal bones while Janelle joined Max and went into the kitchenette to sit at the small table.

Sterling and Tonya plopped down at their desks and turned on the surveillance monitors.

Grant sat on the edge of Gale's cot. He put a warm compress on her eyes and said, "Just lie still and don't worry, it should only be temporary."

"Thank God. I thought for sure I'd never see again." Gale could hear whimpering across the room. "Is that Jasmine?"

"And Luna."

"Poor things are taking it pretty hard."

"So you have no idea what happened to Finn or Ash?"

Gale shook her head. "Only that their horses were dead."

Tonya was close enough to overhear Gale and Grant and called Jasmine and Luna over. "There's a good chance if Finn and Ash are out there, we might be able to see them on our cameras."

Soon everyone but Gale gathered around Tonya and Sterling's desks.

Maya pulled up a chair so Little Rook and Kelly could sit on her lap and watch.

Each screen was subdivided into four black and white smaller screens enabling them to spot as much activity as possible.

Sterling and Tonya reviewed the screens and advanced to the next images.

The blizzard made the screens look like bad reception on a television set.

Sterling was about to press the button on his keyboard when Max said, "Wait, I saw something!" He leaned over Sterling's shoulder and pointed at the screen.

"Oh my God!" Tonya shouted. "It's them!"

Sterling leaned in closer and stared at the two figures caught in the snowstorm. "No, that's not Finn and Ash."

"Then who is it?"

The interior of the Quonset hut suddenly went pitch dark.

"Great," Grant said. "There goes our power."

39

A PEACEFUL WAY TO GO

Darren was beginning to wonder if he had made a big mistake agreeing to go with Jim Harden. Since leaving the bear's cave, and narrowly escaping with their lives, the weather had only worsened. It was bitter cold hiking up the mountain. The higher they went, the deeper the snow became. His pant legs were crusted over with ice and he wasn't sure if he could feel his toes.

They had passed the point of no return a long time ago so it was futile turning back. At least that is what Harden had told him. Darren knew not to question the man and had full confidence that he knew what he was talking about.

Darren couldn't stop thinking about his mother. It wasn't that he was worried about her. He was more concerned he might never see her again. It was obvious it would not end well if they didn't find shelter soon.

The storm had intensified and it was near impossible to see more than five feet ahead of them. The wind was blowing so hard, Darren felt like a test subject marching into a wind tunnel to see what velocity it would take before he was swept off of his feet.

Harden had tethered them together with a short rope so they wouldn't run the risk of getting separated.

"Shouldn't we stop?" Darren yelled. He expected Harden to turn around but the man kept going.

There was only one way to get Harden's attention.

Darren halted and pulled back on the rope. He could see Harden standing still like a statue in the swirling snow.

"Are you all right?" Darren shouted. He trudged through the snow and came up beside Harden. He looked at the man's face.

It was a mask of ice.

Harden's eyelids were frozen shut.

He had been leading the way with his eyes closed all this time.

"No, no!" Darren screamed. He grabbed Harden by the shoulders and shook the man. "Open your eyes! Don't let us die!"

Harden's legs buckled and he dropped to his knees. He managed to open his mouth. "Sorry, kid."

"You've got to get up!" Darren tried to pull the man to his feet but found he was too exhausted and collapsed in the snow.

As Darren lay there, he felt a peaceful calm. *See, dying is not so bad.*

PART FIVE
NEW HAVEN

40

FIRE FIGHT

Cynthia and Nelson heard the series of booms as they ran through the forest.

"What was *that*?" Cynthia asked.

"They're destroying the camp," Nelson said.

They stopped to catch their breath and looked back.

Cynthia saw tendrils of black smoke through the trees rising in the gloomy sky.

Even though it had begun to rain and was almost dark, Cynthia could see the sweat beading on Nelson's brow. He tucked the shotgun into the crook of his arm so he could massage his shoulder.

"Still hurt?" Cynthia asked.

"Aches like a son of a bitch," Nelson replied. "Sure could use a painkiller right about now."

"Sorry, can't help you there."

"Just my luck," Nelson grumbled.

"I can't believe this is happening," Cynthia said. "What are we going to do?"

"Well, look at the bright side: at least we still have the clothes on our backs.""Nelson, this isn't funny."

"You don't see me laughing." He glanced at the pistol in Cynthia's hand. "Just do us both a favor. If the time comes and you're indecisive of whether or not you're going to use that gun, forget about all that Hippocratic Oath bullshit and shoot the bastard."

"I'm a nurse, Nelson. Not a doctor. That doesn't apply to me."

"Oh. Well you know what I'm saying." Without warning, Nelson grabbed Cynthia by the arm and pulled her down close to the ground.

"What's wrong?" she whispered.

Nelson put his forefinger to his lips.

He used the muzzle of the shotgun to point to a thicket a short distance away.

Cynthia thought for an old man, Nelson must have acute hearing, as the only thing she could hear was the torrential rain coming down through the trees.

They watched as Craig Hoskins and two other men stepped out from behind the bushes. Each man was armed with an assault rifle.

Cynthia was about to stand when she felt Nelson's hand press down on her shoulder.

"Stay down," he told her. "I don't trust this asshole not to turn on us."

"But we're on the same side."

"Don't be so sure."

Hoskins and the men were standing out in the open under the pouring rain.

"What are they doing?" Cynthia asked, wiping the wet from her face. "Don't they know they're making themselves easy targets?"

"That fool Hoskins is going to get them all killed."

"Wasn't there more men with him when they left?"

"Yeah, you're right," Nelson said. He scanned the immediate area and nudged Cynthia. "The others are hiding behind those trees. Do you see them?"

"I do."

"They're setting up for an ambush. Guess Hoskins isn't as dumb as we thought."

Suddenly there was a barrage of heavy machinegun fire as more than a dozen muzzle flashes lit up the forest. Pyrotechnic tracer bullets searching for targets left crisscrossing lines of orange that quickly dissipated. Every time a shot fired, the burst would reveal an image of a shooter for a microsecond.

A string of bullets ripped into the man standing next to Hoskins, riddling his chest and face. The other man took direct hits in the chest and legs.

Hoskins strafed the trees as his men behind the bushes shot blindly into the dark.

"We've got to get out of here," Nelson said. "This way." He pulled Cynthia along and they crawled into the brushwood to get as far away from the bedlam as possible.

Hiding behind a covert, Cynthia and Nelson looked back just as there was a lull in the gunfire.

Hoskins was still on his feet but was swaying and appeared to be wounded.

"I have to give it to him, the guy has grit," Nelson said.

Cynthia heard two hollow pops. "What was that?"

"Grenade launchers," Nelson hissed. "Get down!"

The ground under Hoskins exploded in a loud roar. Mud and debris blew into the pouring down rain. A second burst dispersed another eradicating halo of destructive shrapnel.

Cynthia heard Nelson grunt while bloody bits hailed down all around them.

He tugged her coat sleeve and they silently crept away.

41

NO EXCEPTIONS

Emily and Debra were having a devil of a time wrangling the frightened children through the woods. Every time Debra's kids heard a gunshot or an explosion one of the twin girls would let out a scream. Her two boys had remained relatively quiet during the chaos, thanks mostly to Emily's son, Danny, who was acting like a big brother even though they weren't related and doing his best to keep them calm.

They were all drenched from the deluge and it was difficult to see where they were going in the dark as they made their escape from the men that wanted to kill them.

Emily hoped the moonless night and the pouring down rain would work in their favor and cover their tracks.

"Do you think it's the same ones that attacked us before?" Debra asked, marching closely beside Emily.

"Who else would it be?" Emily put a hand on Danny's shoulder. "We're going to rest for a minute. Gather the children and find a spot out of the rain."

"Sure thing, Mom," Danny said.

Danny and the four kids hunkered under an umbrella of low hanging branches, while Emily and Debra stood on the other side of the tree trunk so they could talk and not be overheard by the children.

"Do you think Danny will be all right after what he did?" Debra asked.

"He seems to be. For now," Emily replied, even though she imagined it must be playing a toll on her son's state of mind knowing he was responsible for killing a person, even if it was the scumbag creep Terrell.

But what did she expect living in New Haven? She knew sooner or later the violent environment would affect Danny, though she never dreamed her son would have to resort to what he had done in order to save her from such an evil man.

"Are you sure this is the way to Ernie Mason's place?"

"To tell you the truth, I can't say for certain," Emily confessed.

"Do you think the homesteaders even know what's going on?"

"They would have to be deaf not to have heard the ruckus."

"We need to get these kids to some proper shelter," Debra said.

"Yeah, we've rested enough."

Emily and Debra stepped around the tree trunk.

Two figures stood in the pouring down rain, pointing their machineguns at the children.

"Please, don't shoot," Emily said, raising her hands.

Debra put her arms protectively around her boys and the twins. "For God's sake, they're only children."

"Shut up," said the taller man.

"Are we really doing this?" the other man said.

"You heard Pierce. No survivors. That means no exceptions."

"Stop! Don't do this!" Emily screamed, pulling Danny behind her. "For the love of God, think what you're doing!"

The men exchanged looks then raised their weapons.

42

EARNING THEIR TRUST

Even before Higgins reached the New Haven camp he could smell the smoldering rumble and knew he was too late. He made sure Pierce and his men were no longer lurking in the vicinity before stepping into the clearing. Every cabin had been leveled to the ground. If there had been anything of any value inside the dwellings, the marauders had made sure it was destroyed.

It was like stumbling onto a Third World village after a genocide attack.

Higgins looked around but didn't see any bodies. He was certain Pierce wouldn't bother taking any prisoners, which meant everyone in the camp must have gotten away and fled into the forest; a wise decision as they were likely outgunned by the heavily armed mercenaries.

Sure the residents had the advantage being familiar with the terrain but knowing where to hide was no defense against an aerial assault of propelled grenades.

Higgins wished he could have brought more weapons but he could only carry so much and needed to be fast on his feet in case of a sudden altercation.

He had a 12-gauge short barrel Remington 870 combat shotgun slung across his back and was carrying a fully loaded M27 Infantry Automatic Rifle along with a tactical vest with six 30-round rifle magazines and four 15-round pistol magazines for the Glock 19 holstered on his hip.

He heard the staccato of heavy machinegun fire off in the distance. He figured Pierce's men had caught up to some stragglers and were engaging them in a gun battle.

Then came a loud explosion and the gunfire ceased.

Higgins cut a path through the trees in a direction he hoped would not lead him directly into the hands of the mercenaries. He was getting soaked from the rain cascading down the tall spruce as he forged on. He could hear pinecones falling through the branches and splashing into puddles on the ground.

He had covered maybe two clicks when he heard a male voice tell someone to shut up somewhere up ahead in the dark.

Higgins stayed low and crept closer.

He spotted two men with guns threatening a small group of women and children.

"Are we really doing this?" one of the men said.

"You heard Pierce. No survivors. That means no exceptions."

"Stop! Don't do this!" a woman screamed, shielding a small boy. "For the love of God, think what you're doing!"

Higgins lowered his assault rifle on the ground and drew his Glock out of the holster. Without hesitation, he stepped forward with his handgun extended and shot both men in the head. They jerked forward and fell facedown into the mud.

One woman screamed, startled by the gunshots.

"It's okay," Higgins said, lowering his handgun. "You're safe now."

"Who are you?" the other woman asked.

"I'm Special Agent Higgins with the DOJ. I came here to help."

"All by yourself?"

"Not exactly. What are your names so I know who I'm talking to?"

"My name is Emily Waters. This is my son, Danny."

"And you?" Higgins asked the woman who had screamed earlier.

"I'm Debra Stevens and these are my children."

"You said you work for the DOJ?" Emily asked.

"That's correct," Higgins replied.

"Then you were here before."

"That's right."

"You were going to arrest us and break up our families."

"Not this time. You have to trust me. The other man that was here before, the one called Pierce, he's come back with a small army of mercenaries to wipe you all out."

"And why should we believe you?" Emily asked.

"Because I'm the only hope you have of staying alive."

43

ARMED TO THE TEETH

Even though his cabin could be a one-hour trek away from New Haven depending on the speed of the hiker, Ernie Mason could still hear the explosions in the distance and knew it could only mean one thing.

The DOJ agents had returned to finish the job they had originally set out to do; and that was to hunt down every criminal in the community and bring them back to stand trial in a so-called justice system in which everyone would be found guilty and made to serve life-time prison sentences.

Mason figured it would probably be easier if they just killed everyone and save the government the trouble. By the sounds of it, that was exactly what they were doing.

He stood in his doorway and watched the nighttime rain coming down.

A stream ran along the edge of his small front yard where he would hone tools and weapons on his stationary bike grinder.

Mason had purposely constructed his cabin out of mortared river rock and tucked the structure into the hillside so he could always see who might be approaching, like the four figures coming out of the trees. As they waded across the brook, Mason saw they all had hunting rifles.

The men came into the yard and stopped ten feet away from the front of the cabin.

"We all knew this day would come," Mason said. "Now it has."

"Do we take the fight to them? Like before?" the man named Peterson asked.

"Not this time. Not until we know how many there are."

"Want us to scout around and see if we can find out?"

"Better spread the word to the others. Tell them to get their families to high ground. Then we'll regroup at the designated spot."

The men dispersed and went their separate ways.

Mason stepped inside the lantern-lit cabin.

He went over to a table arrayed with an assortment of different style knives. He picked a satchel up off the floor, laid it on the tabletop, and began to reverently place the knives inside the bag. Another already filled duffle was on another table, which he planned to hide in the woods along with the other bag. He scanned the walls and decided to leave the throwing axes and machetes.

Long before Mason had escaped to the Canadian wilderness and decided to homestead in the Yukon Territory, he had always had a thing for knives, even as a kid, and always carried a knife on him at all times, even if it was only a pocketknife.

Tonight, Ernie Mason was armed to the teeth.

44

SURVIVALIST WIVES

Higgins knew he shouldn't have given the women and children false hope by promising he was going to be able to protect them from Pierce and his mercenaries, but he figured it was the only way he was going to gain their trust.

He had suggested they move away from the two dead men he had just shot.

Debra used her body to shield her children's eyes and ushered the little ones under a tree to shelter away from the rain. Emily's son, Danny, glanced at the bodies facedown in the mud with an unreadable expression on his face before joining the others.

"So were you hiding when I found you?" Higgins asked Emily.

"No. We were told to go to Ernie Mason's place."

"Really." Higgins didn't know how to react. Mason and his men had foiled his first mission with Pierce and was the reason Pierce had returned seeking revenge for being disgraced.

"We got a little turned around but it should be that way," Emily said, pointing her finger toward a dark path through the trees.

"Are you sure?"

"Pretty sure."

"That's good enough. Do either of you know how to handle a gun?"

Emily looked at him like he was the most moronic person on the planet. "Don't forget our husbands were survivalists."

"What was I thinking?" Higgins said. "Are you comfortable with the shotgun?"

As soon as Higgins gave Emily the Remington, she ratcheted the slide pump.

Debra was quick to make sure the Glock was fully loaded when the gun was given to her by inspecting the clip and slamming it back inside the handgrip.

"Okay then," Higgins said. "Lead the way."

Emily marched ahead with Danny right behind. Debra made sure her children walked in pairs to close up the gaps as Higgins guarded the rear. He wasn't sure how far back their pursuers might be or if they were even being followed.

One thing was for sure. Higgins and the two women were hardly a match up against a band of highly trained gunmen. Their best chance was to join up with Mason and his fellow homesteaders.

Even though they might think otherwise and shoot Higgins on sight.

45

A DEAR FRIEND

Cynthia could tell the old man was fatigued by the way he kept taking short, raspy breaths and had shortened his steps to a staggering walk.

"Nelson, we really need to stop."

"No, we have to keep going."

The rain had let up but the saturated branches were still shedding fat raindrops that kept plopping annoyingly down on her head. Cynthia suspected it was only a brief lull in the storm and it would soon start up again, certainly not enough time for them to dry out, as they were both drenched and chilled to the bone.

"Is it your shoulder?"

"No, no, it's fine."

"Let me take a look," Cynthia said, wishing he wasn't so stubborn and would listen to reason. She knew if they kept going at this pace, he would literally run himself into the ground.

"We're almost there," Nelson gasped and tripped in the dark. The shotgun slipped out of his hand as he fell to the ground.

Cynthia knelt beside Nelson and tucked the pistol into her belt so she could use both hands to open his jacket. She expected to see blood on the shoulder of Nelson's shirt but there wasn't any. She opened his coat wider and saw the lower portion of his shirt was soaked with blood. She lifted his shirt and saw blood seeping steadily out of a round hole in his side the size of a silver dollar.

"Oh my God, Nelson, why didn't you say something?" Cynthia took her gloves out of her jacket pocket, placed them over the weeping wound, then grabbed Nelson's hand and put it on the compress. "Hold this."

"Where's my gun?" Nelson said.

Cynthia felt around the wet ground until she found his weapon. "It's right here." She laid the shotgun next to the old man.

"Now get going," Nelson ordered.

"I'm not leaving you!"

"I'll only slow you down."

"No! Absolutely not!"

"Get to Mason's. He'll send someone back for me."

"Nelson, I won't—" Cynthia paused when she heard gunfire not too far away.

"You don't have much time. Go, Goddamn it!" Nelson cursed.

Cynthia leaned down and kissed him on the cheek. "Love you, you old bastard."

"Yeah, love you, too. Now get," Nelson said.

Cynthia stood and didn't look back as she started off through the trees in the dark.

She hadn't gone more than a hundred yards before her emotions got the better of her and she broke down in tears, struggling if she had done the right thing by not telling Nelson that his wound was fatal and he would be dead soon. Judging by the proximity of the hole in his side, the jagged piece of metal had perforated his liver.

But she realized it wouldn't have made a bit of difference when she heard the discharge of his shotgun in the night followed by the rapid reply of machinegun fire.

PART SIX
NORTH STAR
WEATHER STATION

46

SNOW CAVE

Darren opened his eyes and had no idea where he was. He could hear a fire crackling and smell wood smoke, which was drifting up through a hole in a ceiling of ice.

He turned his head and saw two figures squatting on the other side of the flames with their backs turned to him. "Hello? How did I get here?"

When the two men stood, Darren was surprised to see they were so short. They couldn't have been more than five-feet tall and were both wearing animal skins.

Darren's first thought was that he had been rescued by a couple of indigenous Inuit Eskimos. That is until he saw their faces. "What the...who are you?"

"Me Finn," one of the ape-faced men said. He pointed to the other man. "Him Ash."

"Where's Jim?"

"Who?" Finn said.

"Jim Harden. He and I were together."

"I'm right here," a voice said.

Darren sat up. He turned and saw Harden entering the snow cave with a small bundle of branches in his arms.

"I see you've met our saviors, Finn and Ash," Harden said. "They're part of that prehistoric tribe I told you about that lives at the weather station. They dug us out of the snow and brought us here." Harden knelt by the fire to warm his hands. "It's stopped snowing so as soon as you're up to it, we can head out. But first, you're going to want something to eat."

Darren watched as Finn skewed a skinned rabbit and placed it over the fire while Ash carved a sharp point on a stick with a notched end and added the arrow to a small batch lying next to his longbow.

"So how in the world did they find us?" Darren asked, amazed by the primitive men's survival skills.

"Luck, I suppose. They were caught in the storm just like us."

47

SNOWBALL FIGHT

Max opened the Quonset hut's back door and let out a loud whistle when he saw the exit blocked by a wall of snow.

"Good thing you decided to store the snow shovels in here instead of the shed," Morgan said, standing next to the big man.

"Better to be prepared I always say," Max said.

They went over into the storage area next to the lockers and grabbed a couple of snow shovels. Max went first and began chopping away at the snow with the edge of his shovel until he could toss each scoopful out of the way while Morgan hung back and widened the pathway.

The task took them close to thirty minutes by the time Max reached the edge of the deck and had a clear view of the sheer snow-covered mountain face stretching up to the high peak behind the trestle tower.

Janelle came out to join them. She congratulated them by saying, "Nice work," and gazed up at the summit. "Will you look at that? I don't think I've ever seen so much snow."

"I'm going to have to clean off those panels," Max said.

"The hell," Janelle said. "You'll do no such thing. Not after that last fall. Next time you might not be so lucky."

"Janelle's right," Morgan said. "You've taken enough headers. Don't worry, I'll do it."

"Thank you, Morgan," Janelle said and smiled. "It's time someone talked some sense into that thick skull of his."

"You're lucky I have a thick skull," Max countered.

"How's your crew doing?" Morgan asked Janelle.

"Look for yourself."

The three went inside and walked the length of the Quonset hut to the front doorway. The primitive tribe had chosen sides and was engaged in a playful snowball fight. Jasmine and Luna stood knee deep in the snow at the base of the stairs while Maya and the two toddlers had the height advantage on the deck. Little Rook and Kelly were having the time of their lives, giddily tossing clumps of snow at the two women below.

"Nice to see them having fun," Morgan said.

"I hope it breaks Jasmine and Luna out of their funk," Janelle said. "They've been inconsolable worrying about Finn and Ash."

A snowball lobbed their way and struck Morgan in the chest. "Oh, yeah!" He bent down and cupped a round ball of snow in his hands. He reared back and pitched it at Jasmine down below. She dodged the throw while Luna unleashed another snowball that splattered on the Quonset hut wall.

"It's dangerous out here," Max scoffed. "I'm staying inside where it's safe." He walked over to the control panel while Morgan and Janelle stepped outside and began bombarding the other two teams with snowballs.

"Any chance we might get back some power?" Christian asked, standing in the kitchenette next to Digger, wolfing down a bowlful of chow from his food dish.

Christian grabbed a pot of boiling water off the camp stove on the counter, poured a cup of instant coffee, and then sauntered over to his desk.

"Let me see." Max replaced a fuse and reset a couple of toggle switches. "How about now?"

The power button on Christian's laptop computer lit up on his desk. "You certainly have the magic touch."

"Yeah, well, that's only residual power. It won't last very long. We still don't have lights or heat. I'm afraid that's the best I can do until we can clear off the solar panels and recharge the system."

"Well at least it will give us a small window to check the surveillance cameras and hopefully spot Finn and Ash."

* * *

Tonya stepped out of the shower stall and wrapped a towel around her body. "I don't care if there wasn't any hot water, it still felt wonderful."

"You could have fooled me. I could hear your teeth chattering in there the whole time," Sterling said, sitting on the edge of their bed in their sleeping quarters in the back room of the modular.

Sterling showered first as he didn't cherish freezing his butt off and was in and out in two shakes while Tonya wanted to take her time lathering up and washing her hair.

He'd thrown on a pair of jeans and a Pendleton shirt and was lacing up his boots when Tonya came over and sat beside him to dry her hair with another towel.

"Want me to see what I can scrounge up in the kitchen?" he asked.

"I could eat," Tonya said, rubbing her head.

"Don't be disappointed if it turns out to be something out of a box. I imagine everything in the mini fridge is spoiled."

"I'm not picky." Tonya went over to the wardrobe cabinet she shared with Sterling to pick out her clothes to wear.

Sterling sauntered through the tiny home past the sitting room and went into the kitchen. He glanced out the window and saw blue sky through the nearby trees. It was going to be a beautiful clear day. Water was dripping down from the eave as the snow on the roof was beginning to thaw.

Once the power was up and running and the two buggies were charged, they would be able to put together a search party and go look for Finn and Ash.

But first he had to find something for them to eat. He opened the kitchen cabinet and saw a large bag of cereal and a box of powdered milk on a shelf, which he grabbed along with two bowls.

"Did you find anything good?" Tonya called out from the bedroom.

"That's up for debate," Sterling answered back then muttered to himself, "Thank God you're not picky."

* * *

Grant finished clearing the path between the trees from the Quonset hut to the radio shack. He leaned his snow shovel against the wall next to the front door, undid the straps on his snowshoes and stomped his boots on the mat before stepping inside.

"How are you feeling?" he asked, closing the door.

"Much better," Gale said, sitting in a side chair next to Sasha lying in front of the potbelly stove. "I can see better now."

"Make sure you wear sunglasses next time you go outside."

Gale reached down and kneaded the fur on the dire wolf's back. "Aye aye, Captain. Anything you say."

"Gale, this isn't a joke," Grant snapped. "You could have gone blind."

"I know, I know, I'm sorry. I didn't mean to upset you. Come and sit with me."

Grant pulled the other side chair over to the wood-burning stove and sat down. He reached over and took Gale's hand. "No, I'm sorry. I didn't mean to—" but then he stopped when Sasha let out a menacing growl.

"What is it, girl?" Gale asked.

The floor under their feet trembled as the radio shack's walls shook.

48

THE CROSSING

Leaving the life-saving snow cave behind, Harden was relieved to see the sun shining brightly in the cloudless, pastel blue sky.

"Wow, the weather up here can change on a dime," Darren said, traipsing next to Harden as they followed Finn and Ash through the snow.

"I'll say." Harden could hear running water up ahead through the trees.

Finn and Ash stood on a large boulder overlooking a fast-flowing stream. It was maybe fifty feet to the opposite bank.

Harden approached the edge of the stream and could see cobblestones on the keel-shaped bottom through the crystal clear water. It had to be at least ten feet deep in the middle. Attempting a crossing in just two feet of water moving at this rate could sweep a person off of their feet. The last thing Harden wanted was their journey to end tragically with one of them falling in and drowning.

Finn pointed upstream to more snow-covered boulders spaced apart in the swift current that might serve as large stepping-stones. "We cross there," Finn said.

They walked along the bank and stopped at the proposed crossing point.

"So who goes first?" Harden asked.

"I will," Darren said.

"No! Ash go!" Finn put out his hand for Ash to give him the bow and arrows.

"Okay," Harden said. "Who's next after that?"

"Him," Finn said, pointing to Darren. "Then you."

"All right." Harden wasn't used to taking orders, especially from a primitive man, but figured Finn had a legitimate reason for selecting the order in which they should cross.

Ash ran and jumped up onto the first boulder. The surface was slippery but he stayed low and nimbly leapt across a six-foot span to the next large rock.

"He makes it look so easy," Darren said.

Harden had to admit he was impressed by Ash's athletic grace and made the crossing appear effortless.

Ash cleared three more boulders and vaulted onto the opposite shore. He raised his arms and waved for the next person.

"You're up next," Harden said. "Want me to take your backpack?"

"No thanks, I can manage." Darren grabbed his shoulder straps to steady his pack and ran at the first boulder. He used the toes of his boots to propel him up the side of the rock and landed on his hands and knees. He slowly stood, careful not to slip and fall.

"Nice and easy!" Harden yelled so as to be heard over the rushing water.

Darren leaped to the next boulder. This time he landed on his feet and appeared more confident.

"You got this!" Harden shouted, urging Darren on.

The young man jumped to the next boulder. He had two more to go before reaching the opposite bank.

Harden was about to shout out words of encouragement when he noticed the boulder Darren was about to leap onto was moving.

"Darren! Look out for—" but he was too late: Darren had already jumped.

The boulder waded toward the pebbly beach, widening the gap for Darren to clear and he fell in the turbulent water. He went under and fought his way up to the surface.

Ash dashed into the shallows. He grabbed the young man by the backpack before he could be swept downstream and dragged him out of the water.

Harden watched the boulder come ashore and couldn't believe his eyes.

The gigantic armadillo was the size of a compact car and wore a protective armored tortoise-style carapace made up of hexagonal bony plates. Even the top of its head was covered with a plated cap.

At first glance, the docile creature didn't seem to pose much of a threat.

Until Harden saw Finn form a fist and swing his arm in a downward motion as a signal to Ash on the other side of the stream.

"What does that mean?" Harden yelled to Finn.

Harden looked back across the water.

That's when he noticed the armadillo's six-foot long tail with a spiked club on the end dragging on the ground. The animal approached Ash and Darren at an angle and swung its tail like a medieval weapon.

Ash pushed Darren out of the way before the lethal club struck the young man in the head.

Harden dropped his backpack. He slipped the strap of his rifle off his shoulder and lined up a shot at the armadillo.

Before he could pull the trigger, Finn raced over and pulled down the gun barrel. "What are you doing?" Harden protested. "That thing's going to kill them."

Finn shook his head and pointed.

The armadillo had turned away from Darren and Ash and was ambling into the woods. That's when Harden realized the creature wasn't being aggressive but was only protecting itself.

If Finn hadn't intervened, Harden would have killed the otherwise docile animal for nothing.

"Thanks, Finn. For stopping me," Harden said. He slung on his backpack and rifle. He tackled the first boulder and jumped to the next. Finn was right behind as they made their way across the stream.

49

AVALANCHE

The hungry sabertooth followed the goat tracks up the mountain but when the nimble creatures began to tackle a sheer cliff, the big cat was forced to find a different route.

Led by the oldest and largest female, the three young males, another female and two kids headed straight up, jumping from one precarious ledge to another, their double split hooves enabling them to balance miraculously on the icy granite.

Having conquered the climb near the peak, a long horned ram stood on the edge of a cornice and watched the sure-footed herd ascending while the predator forged a parallel way up through the deep snow on the flank of the mountain.

The sun radiated down on the snow pack as a gusty wind swirled a misty cloud of white around the ram.

One by one, the mountain goats reached the top and congregated on the snowy overhang. They stared across the ridge at the sabertooth cat chest deep in the snow, moving slowly in their direction.

A slab of ice cracked like a loud gunshot.

The cornice gave way as the crown fractured beneath the mountain goats and the animals tumbled into the sliding wet snow gaining momentum as it gathered mass, becoming an unstoppable force of destruction.

The gigantic surge of snow flowed all the way down the mountain slope creating a massive cloud of powder as the avalanche plowed down the standing timber in its path, demolishing the radio shack, knocking down the trestle tower, and burying both the tiny home and the Quonset hut.

50

RESCUE PARTY

Even though it had been a while since Harden had been to the weather station, he was beginning to recognize the terrain. Finn and Ash had picked up the pace hiking up through the trees.

"They must be anxious to get home," Darren said, doing his best to keep up.

"Can you blame them?" Harden replied.

"Maybe we should ask them to slow down."

"Not a chance. As long as we keep them in sight, we'll be okay." Just as Harden spoke, the two primitive men broke into a run and dashed up an incline and disappeared. "Well, so much for that. Come on, we better catch up."

The two jogged up the grade with their heavy backpacks. They were almost to the top of the rise when they heard Finn scream out in anguish.

Harden and Darren rushed out of the trees and saw Finn and Ash standing on a colossal snowdrift peppered with debris from the forest floor and splintered tree branches.

"My God, what happened here?" Darren said.

"There's been an avalanche. If I'm not mistaken the weather station is just on the other side. Leave your pack and bring something to dig with," Harden said, shrugging his backpack and taking out his folding shovel.

They climbed up the snowbank.

Harden couldn't believe it was the same place.

The avalanche had caused a landslide of boulders to come crashing down and all the surrounding trees had been leveled to the ground.

He couldn't see any standing structures except the concave roof of the Quonset hut, which looked like a giant tin can on its side buried in the snow, and a few twisted metal pieces from the trestle tower. He looked over expecting to see the radio shack but the building was no longer there.

"There must be people in there," Darren said, pointing to Finn and Ash who had found tree limbs to use as tools and were feverishly digging at the front entrance of the Quonset hut.

"Let's give them a hand," Harden said.

Darren ran over with his shovel and began scooping out the snow. Finn had thrown aside his stick and was digging with his hands.

Harden banged on the side of the metal wall and yelled, "Anyone inside? Can you hear me?"

Muffled voices answered from inside the Quonset hut.

"Thank God, they're still alive," Darren shouted.

Harden heard someone call to them from a short distance away. He turned and saw Grant Olsson and Gale Vincent with their dire wolf, Sasha, coming towards them through the snow.

"Harden, what are you doing here?" Grant asked.

"Came hoping to get some medical supplies. Didn't expect this."

"The whole damn mountain came down," Gale said.

"You're lucky you weren't in the radio shack," Harden said.

"That's it. We were."

"How'd you manage to escape?"

"By running like hell!" Gale said.

"We dug out the snow, you can open the door!" Darren yelled.

The door creaked inwardly.

Jasmine and Luna were the first to come out. They clambered up the snow when they saw Finn and Ash. The women hugged their mates, laughing with joy and crying at the same time.

Max stepped out. "Jesus, it sounded like we got hit by a freight train."

"Pretty close," Grant said. "Anyone hurt?"

"Surprisingly, no."

"How are Little Rook and Kelly?"

"They were a little shaken up but Maya calmed them down." Max stepped out so Janelle could squeeze into the doorframe. She looked up. "What's it look like up there?"

"We lost pretty much everything," Gale said.

"Sorry to hear that," Morgan said, coming out next. "I guess we were lucky there wasn't much damaged in here."

Christian came out, followed by Digger. The chocolate Lab scampered up and raced over to Sasha.

"Who would have thought this old relic could stand up to an avalanche," Christian said with a smile, patting the front wall of the Quonset hut like he was the proud owner.

Gale waited for a moment before saying, "What's taking Sterling and Tonya so long?"

"They're not in here," Christian replied. "They're at the modular."

"Oh my God," Gale gasped. "The tiny home!"

"I don't remember a tiny home," Harden said.

"It was built after you were last here."

"So where is it?"

"Under that!" Gale pointed to the razed timber piled next to the Quonset hut.

"Everybody! We need to get them out before they run out of air!" Grant shouted.

Max rushed back inside the Quonset hut and came out with snow shovels.

"Where do we start digging?" Harden asked.

"Let me mark it off. There's only a front door and some windows," Gale said.

Max and Grant started clearing away debris while Gale grabbed up some broken branches and scurried in a rectangular pattern, placing stakes in the snow where she believed the perimeter of the tiny home might be.

"We don't have much time," Grant yelled to everyone.

Max, Grant, and Harden worked the area at one end while Gale, Darren, and Morgan dug where they believed was the side of the tiny home.

Christian, Finn, and Ash continued to drag the logs away with the help of Jasmine and Luna. Maya made sure Kelly and Little Rook stayed out from under foot.

They had dug down six feet when Grant yelled out, "The roof's caved in!"

Max crouched and used his shovel to chisel a hole in the snow. "I found the door. It's pretty demolished. There's an opening but it's too small for me to fit through."

"How about Finn or Ash?" Grant asked.

"Yeah, they could squeeze in."

Grant yelled out their names and Finn and Ash came running. "We need you to find Sterling and Tonya."

Finn jumped down first.

Ash stayed where he was as there wasn't room for him below.

Grant looked up and saw Janelle.

"He'll need this," she said and tossed down a flashlight.

"Good thinking." Grant switched on the flashlight and passed it to Finn. "Here. Use this to see inside."

Finn took the flashlight and wormed his way through the small crawl space in the doorway.

"We've made it down by one of the windows," Morgan yelled.

"Can you see inside?" Grant yelled back.

"No, it's too dark. Wait, I see a light."

"That would be Finn."

Grant climbed out of the hole. He saw Digger and Sasha clawing out a big bowl of snow in the middle of the staked out area. "Hey, Christian, I can't believe this! Sasha and Digger are..."

The ground opened up under the dog and dire wolf.

One second they were there, the next they were gone.

"Holy shit!" Grant ran over and looked down.

Sasha and Digger had fallen through the damaged roof into one of the rooms of the modular. Tonya was down on one knee checking the pair to make sure they were unhurt.

"Well, I'll be darned," Sterling said, standing next to his wife and grinning up at Grant. "Look who decided to drop in and pay us a visit."

PART SEVEN
NEW HAVEN

51

BLADES AND BULLETS

Cynthia hadn't heard gunfire in the past hour but that didn't mean the mercenaries weren't close by.

It was daybreak and the rain had stopped. Judging by the early morning sun filtering down through the trees and the hint of rainbow in the clearing sky, the storm had moved on.

She wished it was still nighttime and raining because now she was an easy target out in broad daylight. Which is why she had to hurry to get to Mason's cabin before she ended up in a sharpshooter's crosshairs.

She felt guilty for leaving Nelson behind though she was certain his wound from the fragmented bomb was fatal. She prayed his death had been swift.

Holding the pistol by her thigh, she kept to a brisk pace, trying her best not to make too much noise. She had just traversed around some rocks when she heard voices from behind. She stepped over to a tall fern and ducked out of sight.

"I'm telling you, Baker, they went this way." A mercenary appeared, his eyes searching the ground. He pointed at the muddy trail. "See, I told you."

Cynthia saw a second mercenary come into view and gaze down at the same spot. "God damn, Carver. Sure you're not part bloodhound."

"Damn straight I am."

Both men swiveled at the hips and pointed their guns in Cynthia's direction.

"Show us your hands and come out," Baker said.

Carver cocked his machinegun. "It's either that or we use our weed eaters."

"Okay, okay, don't shoot." Cynthia stood up and raised her left hand, making sure they couldn't see the pistol in her other hand hidden behind the fern leaves.

"Let's see both hands," Baker said.

"Promise you won't shoot?"

"The other hand," Carver said, holding his weapon to his shoulder and lining Cynthia up in his sights. "Not going to tell you again."

"Very well." She knew if they saw the pistol in her hand they would gun her down for sure. Slowly, her fingers began to let go...

Baker's head jerked and he took an awkward step toward the other man.

"What the hell?" Carver said when he saw the handle of the knife sticking out of Baker's neck.

Cynthia raised her pistol and shot Carver.

The bullet entered his right eye, bored through his brain and shattered the back of his skull in an explosive crimson mist. His knees folded and he went down.

Mason stepped out of the trees, wearing a belt sheathed with a dozen throwing knives. He walked up to Baker and yanked the knife out of the dead man's throat. He wiped the blade on Baker's vest, placed it back in the empty sheath, and after looking at the other man on the ground, glanced over at Cynthia. "Nice shot."

"Jim's a good teacher," Cynthia said.

"Too bad Harden's not here," Mason said. "We could really use him right about now. Anyway, we better not stand around."

Cynthia tucked the pistol in her belt and followed Mason.

52

BOXED IN

"That's Mason's cabin," Emily said as they came out of the trees.

"Let's hold up for a second." Higgins still wasn't sure what kind of reception he could expect from Mason. He doubted the man would come out to greet him with open arms. Debra and her four children waited patiently next to Emily and Danny for Higgins to make up his mind.

The running stream in front of the cabin looked shallow enough for them to carry the children across. Higgins didn't like the idea of being out in the open but didn't see any other way. "Emily, do you think you and Danny could help Debra with the children?"

"Sure."

"Good. I'll keep a lookout while you guys get across." Higgins walked over to the edge of the stream and kept his back to the cabin so he could keep an eye on the tree line.

Emily put one of the twins on her shoulders. Danny let the other child climb onto his back while Debra gathered her other two children in her arms and they all crossed the narrow stream.

Higgins kept his M27 pointed at the trees and stepped backwards across the water.

Once they were lowered to the ground, the children stood around their mother.

"Something doesn't feel right," Emily said.

"Why, what's wrong?" Higgins asked.

"The cabin door's open."

Higgins came over, pushed the door the rest of the way with the muzzle of his rifle and took a quick glance inside. "There's no one here."

"The children are exhausted," Debra said. "Let me take them in so they can lie down."

"Sure, go ahead."

"Thanks." Debra shooed her children into the cabin.

"Danny, go get some rest," Emily said.

"I want to stay out here and help keep watch."

"Maybe later."

"All right." Danny gave his mother a grim smile and went inside.

"This must be tough," Higgins said.

"If you only knew," Emily replied. "It's been especially hard on him."

"How so?"

"I'd rather not talk about it right now."

"Fair enough," Higgins said. "I'm not so sure staying here is such a good idea. We're pretty much boxed in."

"What? We're not going to wait for Mason?" Emily rested the short barrel shotgun in the crook of her arm.

"That's the thing. I don't know if—" Higgins stopped in mid sentence.

"What is it?" Emily asked, aiming the shotgun at the trees across the creek.

"We better go in." Higgins waited for Emily to slip through the door before following her inside the cabin. He pushed the door closed. "Everyone! On the floor!" Higgins grabbed a table and flipped it on its side. "Get the children behind the table." He crawled over and knocked another table over.

A barrage of gunfire assaulted the front of the cabin, blasting out the windows and riddling the door with holes.

The children screamed and began crying. Debra wrapped her arms around them like a protective mother bird shielding her chicks under her wing.

"How many do you think there are?" Emily asked Higgins, hunkered behind a table with her son.

"I'm not sure." It was difficult for Higgins to determine the number of shooters outside as they had all been firing at the same time. When there was a lull in the gunfire, Higgins figured they were reloading their weapons; or worst still, contemplating an assault with their grenade launchers. Higgins scrambled over to a window and peeked through the broken glass.

Four men splashed across the creek, firing their machineguns.

"They're making a run at the cabin!"

Bullets ripped through the shattered windows, blasting chunks out of the back wall, and knocking down Mason's assortment of axes and machetes.

"Emily, take the other window." Higgins stood and began firing. He stopped the man in the middle who was the first one out of the water, running past the stationary grinder. Slugs hit the man in his protective body armor. He slowed for a moment then kept on running.

Higgins aimed lower and cut the man off at the knees.

Emily fired her shotgun at a mercenary charging the door. The close range blast picked him up off his feet and sent him sprawling to the ground.

A man kicked in the door with his boot. He was about to strafe the room when Debra lunged out from behind the table and swung a long handled axe. The blade cleaved into the side of his head. He toppled over and crashed onto the floor.

The last man was hanging back, getting ready to fire his grenade launcher.

"Everyone! Get out!" Higgins yelled. He stepped outside and fired at the mercenary as Debra and Emily ushered the children out.

The man took a bullet to the throat but not before launching the grenade.

Everyone dove onto the ground.

A loud, fiery explosion and the cabin blew up in a black cloud of smoke.

Higgins was the first on his feet. He helped Emily up. Debra was busy checking to make sure her children had not been hurt by the blast.

"You okay, Mom?" Danny asked.

"I should be asking you that question," Emily said, placing her hand on her son's shoulder and pulling him close. She looked at Higgins. "Tell me that's the last of them."

"I wish I could. I'm sure Pierce has more men with him."

"So what do we do? We obviously can't stay here."

"What the hell did those bastards do?" a voice yelled.

Higgins spun around and pointed his rifle at the two figures crossing the creek.

"Thank God," Emily said. "It's Mason and Cynthia."

"You remember me?" Higgins said, directing the question to Mason.

"As a matter of fact, I do. Are these men yours?" Mason said, motioning to the dead mercenaries lying in his yard.

"No, they're not. I came here to warn you."

"Well, judging by these bodies, you did much more than that."

"Are any of you hurt?" Cynthia asked, walking over to inspect the children.

"Maybe some scrapes and cuts," Debra said.

Mason walked into the woods, and less than a minute later, returned with two duffle bags. When he dropped them on the ground the contents made a metallic sound.

"What's in there?" Higgins asked.

Mason leaned down and unzipped one of the bags.

Higgins looked inside. "Knives? Seriously?"

"What did you expect, gold bars?" Mason said.

53

IMPATIENTLY WAITING

Navy pilot Mike Fenton didn't like sitting in the floatplane's cockpit and having to wait. He preferred a fast extraction where he would make the drop and shortly after the tactical team would be back aboard and they would be in the air heading back to base.

Not this time.

For hours he heard explosions and gunfire tapering off in the distance. He had no idea what was going on or if the men he had transported were in trouble. Special Agent Higgins had instructed Fenton they keep strict radio silence in case Pierce and his men might be listening in.

Fenton felt like the pilot in the *Indiana Jones* movie, passing the time while he waited for the archeologist to return to the seaplane. Instead of standing on a pontoon with a fishing pole, Fenton had kept occupied checking and rechecking the gauges on the instrument panel.

He had even started up the twin engines and kept them running for a couple of minutes—mindful of the fuel remaining—before switching them off to ensure they would fire up immediately in the event they needed to make a hasty escape.

Fenton got up from the pilot's seat to stretch his legs.

He went back into the passenger compartment for the umpteenth time. He peeked out one of the windows at the morning sky and no longer saw smoke on the horizon above the trees.

Fenton opened the side hatch and stepped out onto the pontoon. He took a deep breath of the pine-scented air. Even though it wasn't visible, he could smell the smoke.

He unsnapped the flap on his holster and drew his government issue Colt .45. He did a routine check of his weapon and slipped it back in the holster.

Fenton was about to step back into the passenger compartment when he heard a plane's engine steadily approaching.

He jumped down from the pontoon. Landing in six inches of water, Fenton ran up the bank and made his way to the edge of the cove.

An amphibious aircraft sped down the river and lifted off the water. There were no markings on the side of the blue and silver fuselage signifying its origin. Fenton figured it had to be the seaplane that brought Pierce and his mercenaries.

"I'll be damned. Looks like Higgins kicked some ass," Fenton cheered, watching the seaplane soar over the trees and disappear.

54

BREAKING RADIO SILENCE

Cynthia had just finished examining the children when she heard a two-way radio squawk on Higgins' utility belt.

He frowned and muttered, "He knows not to give away his position until he hears from me." Higgins pressed the talk button. "Fenton, stay off this frequency."

"Pierce and his men are gone," Fenton said.

"Can you confirm?"

"I saw their plane takeoff. Do you have any instructions?"

"Hold tight and I'll get back to you."

"Oh my God," Debra shouted. "Did you hear that, kids? The bad men are gone."

Her two boys and the twin girls smiled at their mother.

"Is it really over?" Danny asked Emily.

Emily looked at Higgins.

"If Fenton says he saw them leave then I guess it is."

"Well then, I guess I can call my men in," Mason said. He put his thumb and middle finger in his mouth and let out a shrill whistle.

A dozen homesteaders carrying hunting rifles stepped out of the trees.

"They were out there this whole time?" Higgins asked.

"Actually, they were right behind us when Mason and I arrived," Cynthia said.

"Not always a good idea to show your cards until you know you have a winning hand," Mason said. "Know what I mean?"

"Smart move," Higgins replied.

"I thought so."

"Shame about your cabin."

"I can always build another one," Mason said.

"At least you were able to salvage your knives," Higgins said with a smirk, looking down at the two duffle bags on the ground.

"All one-of-a-kind and handcrafted by yours truly," Mason had to remind the agent.

"So what happens now?" Cynthia asked.

"Well, now we—" but Higgins didn't get a chance to finish his sentence when gunfire erupted from the woods on the other side of the creek. He was struck in the chest and fell in the dirt.

Three of Mason's men went down next.

Debra tackled her children to the ground, protecting them with her body.

Emily grabbed Danny's hand and they ran to a nearby tree. Halfway there, Emily took a bullet in the leg. She managed to hobble behind the tree trunk and hide with Danny.

Mason knelt, picked up one of his bags for a shield as slugs struck and ricocheted off the metal blades inside.

Pierce and six of his mercenaries stepped out from behind the trees, unleashing a sweeping barrage of machine gunfire, striking four more of Mason's men. But not before three mercenaries got caught in a crossfire and were shot dead.

A mercenary pointed his weapon at Debra and her children.

He dropped like a sack of wet laundry when a throwing knife struck him in the temple.

The remaining men on both sides continued firing at one another like Civil War infantrymen in a close range volley until there was only one man standing—Pierce.

Mason pulled another throwing knife from his belt and was about to heave it at Pierce, but then he froze when he saw the other man pointing his weapon at him.

"Drop the knife," Pierce ordered.

Mason did as he was told.

"Hands on the top of your head."

Mason complied.

Pierce glared at Cynthia, standing a few feet from Mason.

"Get down on your knees next to your friend. Hands on your head."

Cynthia joined Mason.

Realizing the unpleasant turn in their situation, Debra's children began to cry.

"Shut them up or I will!" threatened Pierce.

Debra did her best to coax the children to be quiet.

"You! Behind the tree! Get over here and bring the kid."

Emily limped out with one hand on Danny's shoulder for support. They came over and got down on the ground next to Cynthia.

Pierce looked down at Higgins, lying still on the ground. He pointed the muzzle of his gun at Higgins' head.

"Why are you still here? We thought you left," Cynthia said.

"Glad to see my little ruse worked. Don't worry. My pilot will be coming back."

"You're nothing but a coward."

Pierce raised his assault rifle at Cynthia. "Coward, huh? It's going to give me great satisfaction knowing I was the one who wiped New Haven off the map; not that it was ever on any map." He pulled back the slide on his weapon. "Any last words?"

"Yeah, I got some," Higgins said, lying flat on his back and looking up from the ground. "How about you go to hell?" and then he fired a single shot.

The bullet bored a tiny hole under Pierce's chin and came out messy, blowing out the top of his skull.

55

HARD DECISIONS

Higgins went to sit up.

"Lie still and let me have a look at you," Cynthia said, kneeling beside him and gently pushing him back on the ground.

"I'm okay, really." Higgins let Cynthia unbutton the front of his shirt so she could see he was wearing his Kevlar bulletproof vest.

She undid the Velcro straps and took a look at the fresh welt on his chest. "That was dead center. My God, you're bruised all over. Good thing you wore body armor."

"Doesn't mean it doesn't hurt like the dickens."

"Here, let me help you up."

Higgins put out his hand and let Cynthia pull him to his feet.

"Jesus," Mason said, as he looked around at all the bodies.

Cynthia immediately went into triage mode. "Mason, I'm going to need you to see if anyone is still alive while I examine Emily."

Mason started with the homesteaders first.

"Let me see your leg," Cynthia said to Emily.

The woman hobbled over and dropped her pants.

"You're fortunate, the bullet only grazed your calf but we have to stop the bleeding. Sit down but keep your legs bent."

"I should have what you need in my medical kit," Higgins said, removing a Combat Lifesaver Bag from his belt. He pulled out a large bandage and started applying pressure to the wound.

Cynthia took out a small bottle of iodine. "This is going to sting."

Emily yelped when Cynthia applied the solution.

"Now for some antibiotic."

Higgins waited until Cynthia was done with the ointment and had put a clotting agent on the cut before he wrapped an elastic emergency trauma bandage around Emily's calf. "There, that should do it," he said.

Danny helped his mother to stand so she could pull up her pants.

"Find a good spot for your mom to sit and rest," Cynthia instructed the boy.

"Cynthia!" A despondent Mason shook his head, signaling he had found no survivors.

"And all for what?" Cynthia said, almost in tears. She glared at Pierce's dead body. "Because this maniac got his feelings hurt?"

"I can't tell you how sorry I am," Higgins said. "I was really hoping I could stop him from hurting anyone."

Mason walked over and joined them. "So what now?"

"As you no longer have homes thanks to Pierce, it looks like the only choice you have is to come back with me," Higgins said.

"Not in your life," Mason hissed. "There's no way in hell that's going to happen."

"What about Emily and her son? I'm sure Debra would want to get her children out of here. Don't they get a say in this?"

Cynthia turned and looked at the two women. "What do you think? Do you want to go with Higgins?"

"What guarantees do we have we won't end up in prison and our kids will be taken away?" Debra asked.

"I'll make sure that never happens. You have my word," Higgins replied.

"Where will we live?" Emily wanted to know.

"Anywhere you want. My uncle is very influential. He'll make sure you're well taken care of."

"What, like a Witness Protection Program?" Emily said.

"Something like that. So, what do you say?"

"We'll do it," Debra said. She looked at Emily for confirmation.

"Yes. Danny and I want to go."

"What about you, Cynthia?"

"I can't leave. Not without Jim and my son."

"I was meaning to ask. Where are they?"

Cynthia knew not to answer truthfully. "Jim took Darren on a long hunting trip. I have no idea when to expect them back."

"You know I have no problem coming back if you should change your mind."

"No. We're staying put."

Mason stood by Cynthia's side. "Thanks for your concern, but we'll be fine."

"Very well." Higgins motioned for those leaving to follow him and they started across the creek.

"Oh, Higgins," Cynthia called out.

Higgins turned around. "Yes?"

"Thanks."

"You're more than welcome," Higgins said and smiled.

Thirty minutes later, Cynthia and Mason were sifting through the smoldering rubble of the cabin when they heard a plane engine passing over the treetops.

Mason gazed at the bodies. "Looks like I have some friends to bury."

"What do you plan to do with the others?" Cynthia asked, referring to Pierce and his men.

"Leave them for the scavengers."

PART EIGHT
NORTH STAR
WEATHER STATION

56

NEW AND IMPROVED

SIX MONTHS LATER...

Morgan uncoupled the charger cable having powered up the last of the dune buggies and gazed around the outpost, amazed at how much they had accomplished.

The trestle tower was back up on its foundation with more efficient solar panels than before, thanks to Max's ingenuity in reclaiming damaged parts.

Even though the metal exterior looked like a beer-drinking giant had crinkled the can, the Quonset hut was still structurally sound having withstood the destructive force of the avalanche.

As Grant and Gale's home was a total loss, it had been decided to build a log cabin in place of the original radio shack as there was plenty of fallen timber to use after the thaw and it would require less hand milling. By building on higher ground they hoped to avoid another natural disaster.

The new greenhouse was twice as big as the previous one, which meant Janelle, Jasmine, and Luna could expect to grow an abundant seasonal harvest of fresh vegetables and berried fruits.

Sterling and Tonya's modular home had suffered some serious damage and much of the portable's building material had been destroyed beyond repair. It made more sense to salvage what they could as an add-on and create a completely new structure.

Five hipparion horses stood in the shade under an overhang, grazing on a pile of prairie grass inside the corral. An adjacent holding pen had been included where Sterling administered veterinarian care for distressed animals so when they recovered they could later be released back into the wild.

Morgan went up the back steps onto the porch and entered the Quonset hut.

"Come sit. I made you a plate," Janelle said, motioning to Morgan's usual spot at the long dining table.

"Thanks." Morgan slid his legs over the bench and sat across from Sterling drinking a cup of coffee.

"Take your time," Sterling said. "Tonya and Christian will be a few more minutes reviewing the surveillance cameras."

"Any idea where you might want to go?" Morgan asked, raising a spoonful of stew meat to his mouth.

"I would like to see how the mammoths are doing."

After Morgan finished eating, he carried his plate over to the kitchen sink. "Thanks again, Janelle."

"My pleasure," Janelle replied.

"I'm ready," Tonya said, getting up from her desk.

"How about you, Christian?" Morgan asked.

"Nothing to report here," Christian said.

Morgan led the way outside and went down the steps to the dune buggies.

Grant and Gale were loading slatted crates onto the flatbed of their utility vehicle.

"Taking a run over?" Morgan asked.

"Thought they could use some produce," Gale replied.

"Tell them we said hi."

"Will do. Where you three off to?"

"Doing our rounds with Dr. Dolittle." Tonya playfully elbowed Sterling.

"This time try and stay out of trouble," Grant said.

"Speak for yourself," Morgan replied, getting behind the wheel as Sterling and Tonya climbed aboard.

57

THE COVE

Grant drove the two-mile distance on what looked like a rutted wagon trail until they reached the two cabins near the riverbank. He parked the dune buggy under the shade of a giant spruce.

"Where is everyone?" Gale said.

"Must be down by the—" but then Grant stopped speaking when he saw a wide trail of blood in the dirt leading around one side of a cabin, like a dead animal—or a person—had been mauled and dragged off by a large predator.

"Oh my God," Gale gasped.

Grant grabbed his hunting rifle and stepped from the buggy.

Gale climbed out of the passenger seat. She walked around the vehicle and gazed down at the ground. "That's so much blood." Gale was about to call out to see if anyone was around when Grant raised his hand to silence her.

"Did you hear that?" Grant threw back the bolt on his rifle and inserted a round in the chamber. "Stay here."

"Not on your life."

Grant and Gale crept to the side of the cabin.

Slashing sounds could be heard from around back.

They caught a whiff of mesquite smoke.

Suddenly, they felt foolish, and stepped around the corner.

Portions of venison were carved up on a table.

Mason stood with his back turned and was hanging meat onto hooks inside of a smokehouse. As soon as he heard footsteps behind him, he turned around. "Hey, you two. I've got choice cuts and jerky whenever you want to barter." Mason couldn't help but notice Grant's hunting rifle pointed in his direction.

"Sorry," Grant said, lowering his weapon. "We saw the blood and thought there was trouble."

"It's from the buck," Mason said. "I know it looks a sight. I haven't had a chance to clean it up."

"That's okay. We don't mind helping out. Where is everyone?" Gale asked.

"Down by the cove."

"Will we see you down there?"

"As soon as I'm done," Mason replied and went back to carving the meat.

Grant and Gale walked around to the front.

While Grant put his rifle back in the dune buggy, Gale found some long branches with bristly pine needles lying on the ground they could use as crude brooms.

It took only a few minutes to smooth a top layer of dirt over the drag marks of dried blood to dissuade the flies. They decided to leave the produce in the back of the dune buggy for now and walk down to the cove.

Yellow daisy and buttercup wild flowers carpeted the hillside on the way to the river. The shoreline was flat rocks and boulders with a horseshoe strip of sandy beach edged around a cove of crystal clear water.

"Hey, everyone!" Gale called out.

Jim Harden and Cynthia Lane were sitting on a blanket and looked over their shoulders. "Come sit with us," Cynthia said.

"Sure is a gorgeous day," Gale said, plopping down beside Cynthia.

Grant looked upriver. He saw Finn and Jasmine riding bareback, Ash and Luna on a second horse.

He turned his attention to the activity in the water. "Looks like everyone's having a good time."

"Oh, yeah," Harden replied, his rifle lying by his side just in case. "That beast of yours sure loves the water."

Little Rook and Kelly were clinging to Sasha's back while the dire wolf waded alongside Maya in the shallows.

Darren ran into the water and dove under the surface. Seconds later, he popped up in front of Maya and splashed her. Giggling, she wiped her face and splashed him back.

"Looks like we have company," Grant said, pointing across the river at five slender-legged camels on the opposite bank. The front of their long giraffe-like necks, bellies, and the backs of their legs were white, the rest of their bodies a light brown. They seemed oblivious to their surroundings as they stretched their heads up into the tree branches to nibble on the low hanging leaves.

Three bear-dogs suddenly charged out of the forest.

The camels took flight and galloped into the river as the carnivores, each weighing more than four hundred pounds, chased after them.

"Everybody, out of the water!" Grant yelled like a frantic lifeguard waving swimmers ashore after spotting a shark's fin headed in their direction.

58

ELSA AND STANLEY

Morgan stopped the buggy on a ridge so they could take in the panoramic view of the lush green valley below.

"There they are," Sterling said, pointing to the single herd of over a dozen woolly mammoths and three Asian elephants, congregating on the shoreline of a pristine lake.

Tonya raised her binoculars to watch the animals. "Oh my God," she said. "I see Elsa and Stanley."

"Can I take a look?" Sterling asked. After Tonya handed him the binoculars, Sterling confirmed one of the Asian elephants was indeed Elsa. The present-day surrogate was standing alongside the prehistoric woolly mammoth, Stanley, which was Elsa's bio-engineered offspring via artificial insemination created during the Cenozoic Project. "They look healthy," he commented.

"Why wouldn't they?" Morgan said. "They survived the winter, there's plenty of food and drinking water to go around."

"Tonya and I worry these animals will one day experience mutation meltdown."

"Which is?" Morgan asked.

"It's a subclass of extinction vortex."

"Again, you've lost me. Mind putting that into layman's terms?"

"That we might have overlooked a deleterious mutation that could eventually eradicate the population."

Morgan started to laugh. "You mean one day they might go extinct."

"Exactly."

"Well, short of a meteor strike," Morgan said, continuing to laugh, "it looks like they'll be around for a while."

Sterling handed Tonya back the binoculars. "Let's go down. I'd like to examine Elsa and Stanley."

"What makes you think they'll let you get near them?" Morgan said.

Tonya smiled at Morgan. "Because Sterling and I assisted Elsa when she gave birth to Stanley."

"And you know what they say," Sterling said.

"No, what's that?" asked Morgan.

"Pachyderms never forget a face."

After a good laugh, they headed down into the valley.

59

BLOOD IN THE SAND

Maya tried to move out of the way of the camels as they ran into the cove to escape the bear-dogs. The leading camel slammed into her, sending her crashing into the water. Darren scooped up Little Rook and Kelly before a second camel could stampede the two youngsters.

Harden grabbed his rifle. He attempted to get to his feet but was knocked back to the ground by a camel that veered to its left and trampled Cynthia.

Sasha charged at the bear-dogs invading the cove.

"Gale! Get Mason and my rifle!" Grant hollered. He ran over to Harden who was lying on the ground.

"Take my rifle, the damn thing broke my arm," Harden yelled and crawled over to Cynthia.

A bear-dog ran straight for Sasha. The dire wolf rose on her hind legs and clashed with the larger animal, their teeth gnashing at each other's faces.

Finn let out a battle cry, using the heels of his feet to spur his horse. Jasmine slipped off the back of the horse, landing in the water next to Maya who was floating facedown on the surface. Finn got the horse to rear up. The front hooves were about to come down on the bear-dog when the carnivore sprang under the horse's belly.

The horse screeched when its intestines spilled out, narrowly missing Finn as his steed fell on its side, splashing into the water.

Ash and Luna clung to the back of their horse and chased after the bear-dog heading up the hill toward the cabins. Drawing his knife from his scabbard, Ash launched himself off the horse and onto the back of the running bear-dog. The primitive man held onto the creature's mane and repeatedly stabbed the beast in the nape of the neck. The jabbing blade finally severed the spinal cord and down it went.

The camels broke ranks and galloped past Gale and Mason running down the hill.

Grant raised Harden's rifle, took aim, but couldn't get a clean shot at the bear-dog scrapping with Sasha. Afraid he might hit the dire wolf, he ran across the sand and into the water. He raised the barrel up in the air and fired off a single round. The loud retort of the gunshot was enough to draw the bear-dog's attention.

Throwing back the bolt, Grant ejected the spent cartridge. He went to ram another bullet into the chamber and the gun jammed.

The bear-dog barreled past Sasha and lunged at Grant.

Another gunshot rang out. The beast's head jerked back and it fell dead in the water. Grant looked over his shoulder and saw Gale holding his rifle.

The remaining bear-dog bolted downstream and disappeared around the bend.

"Mom!" Darren screamed, running to his mother.

"I'm fine," Cynthia said, dazed from being mowed down by the camel but coherent enough to examine Harden's injured arm. "You on the other hand are not and have a compound fracture."

"Cynthia! We need you over here!" Gale shouted, knelt over Maya who was lying on her back, unconscious. Gale pinched Maya's flat nose, put her lips up to the Paranthropus woman's mouth and blew in a lung full of air.

"I need to do chest compressions," Cynthia said, kneeling beside Gale. The nurse put one hand over the other, interlocked her fingers, and began pumping Maya's chest to stimulate her heart and get her breathing again.

Everyone gathered around. Little Rook and Kelly were especially concerned and started crying. Jasmine and Luna stood behind the youngsters, doing their best to comfort them.

"Come on, Maya, wake up," Darren pleaded, standing over the two women trying desperately to revive Maya. Finn and Ash stood off to the side as Grant and Mason watched on.

Alternating mouth-to-mouth and chest compressions, Gale and Cynthia continued to administer CPR. Suddenly, Maya gagged and water spewed out of her mouth.

Cynthia immediately rolled the young woman onto her side so she could expel the rest of the water from Maya's lungs before returning her onto her back.

Maya looked up, slightly embarrassed and gave everyone a silly grin, which evoked a thunderous cheer accompanied by waterworks of joy.

60

A TRIUMPHANT SEND-OFF

The dune buggy crept up behind the herd and stopped about a hundred feet away from the giant creatures. Instead of getting out right away, Sterling, Tonya, and Morgan remained in their seats and observed the woolly mammoths and the three Asian elephants dipping their long trunks into the water. Some would curl their trunks up to shoot water into their mouths while others sprayed their heads and backs.

Four young male woolly mammoths were a short distance away, plowing up huge clumps of vegetation with their long tusks so they could pick it up with the end of their proboscises to feed themselves. Whenever a bull got too close and invaded the other one's space, tusks would clash like swordsmen's sabers backing away from a duel so they could resume furrowing up the soil.

Sterling climbed out and grabbed his medical kit from the cargo bed. "Morgan, you better stay with the buggy while Tonya and I go check on Elsa and Stanley."

"Sure about that?" Morgan replied, resting his hand on the barrel of the shotgun mounted between the front buck seats.

"Maybe he should come," Tonya said. "I know the mammoths have poor eyesight but anything could trigger an attack."

"Which is why I'm more worried about the elephants," Sterling said.

"Then we should approach Elsa first," Tonya said. "Once she feels comfortable with us, she could calm the others and won't mind us looking at Stanley."

They were twenty feet away when one of the elephants turned her head as if having overheard the three talking. There was a look of recognition in the animal's eyes as it moved in a semi-circle. The elephant raised her trunk and trumpeted.

"Well hello, Elsa," Sterling said.

The woolly mammoth standing next to Elsa was almost as tall as his surrogate mother. Stanley had a long fur coat and when he eventually became a full-grown adult, would measure more than twelve feet from the ground to the shoulders and have ten-foot long tusks like the other mammoths. Stanley trumpeted once he saw the familiar faces that were present when he was born.

"Nice to see you too, Stanley."

Both animals lumbered over while the rest of the herd seemed oblivious to the three humans in their midst.

Sterling extended his hand for both the pachyderms to smell.

Elsa snorted water onto Sterling's jacket while Stanley wrapped the end of his trunk around Sterling's right arm and almost tugged him off his feet.

"That's quite the greeting," Tonya laughed. She stepped forward and ran her hand up and down Elsa's trunk.

Elsa dipped her head in a ceremonious bow.

"Please tell your boy to release my husband," Tonya said, smiling up at the elephant.

Elsa brushed against Stanley. The young woolly mammoth got the message and released Sterling's arm.

"Thanks, big guy. For a minute there I thought I was going to have to change my name to Lefty," Sterling quipped. He quickly gave the woolly mammoth a quick visual once-over and was pleased to see the animal in good condition. He didn't need a stethoscope to listen to Stanley's lungs, as his breathing seemed normal; tuberculosis being a common affliction with large land animals.

"That one seems to be having a bit of a problem," Morgan said, pointing to an older female limping away from the water.

"Poor thing is suffering from osteoarthritis," Sterling said. "Most likely her hips and shoulder joints. Eventually, I'm sorry to say, they'll all get it."

"Is there anything you can do?"

"I'm afraid not. We don't have enough medicine to treat her."

"I hate to say it, but isn't it somewhat ironic?" Morgan said.

"There he goes again. What is it this time?" Tonya asked.

"You and Sterling spend over thirty years of your lives bioengineering these creatures and bringing them back from extinction only to see them succumb to natural diseases and die anyway."

"It does seem futile when you put it that way."

"Hence the old adage: Nothing last's forever," Morgan said.

Tonya looked at Sterling. "What do you think? Was it all for nothing?"

"I think you should be asking him that," Sterling replied and cocked his head at Stanley.

The young woolly mammoth raised his trunk and let out a loud bellow, which got the other beasts trumpeting.

Sterling smiled and put his arm around Tonya's shoulders. "Does that answer your question?"

TO THE READER

I hope you enjoyed *DEEP IN THE WILD: MAMMOTH.* If you are interested in reading more of my books and have a proclivity for mutant insects perhaps you might like the *DEATH CRAWLERS* series or if you fancy cryptozoology there is the *CRYPTID ZOO* series, and the megafauna series *DEEP IN THE WILD.* For those of you that like Bigfoot, there are the *MOUNTAIN* books. And let's not forget those monstrous catfish in *SILURID.* If you prefer a novel about detectives investigating the macabre, might I suggest *IN CASE OF CARNAGE?* And if your partiality is short stories, please check out my horror collection *CREATURES.* Just thought I would throw that out there. Happy reading!

ACKNOWLEDGEMENTS

I would like to thank Gary Lucas, Romana Baotic, Nichola Tennick, and the wonderful people working with Severed Press that helped with this book. It's truly amazing how folks who live in the most incredible places in the world can truly enrich our lives. A special thanks to my wonderful daughter and faithful beta reader (and accomplished artist on Fine Art America) Genene Griffiths Ortiz for her enthusiasm and making this so much fun. And of course, I would like to thank you, the reader, for taking the time to share these bizarre and incredible journeys with me.

ABOUT THE AUTHOR

Gerry Griffiths lives in San Jose, California with his wife and their five rescue dogs. He is a Horror Writers Association member. Gerry has over 30 published short stories in various anthologies and magazines, along with his own collection of 22 short stories entitled *Creatures*. He is the author of *In Case of Carnage: A Paranormal Crime Novel* as well as 22 novels published by Severed Press.

Check out other great

Cryptid Novels!

J.H. Moncrieff

RETURN TO DYATLOV PASS

In 1959, nine Russian students set off on a skiing expedition in the Ural Mountains. Their mutilated bodies were discovered weeks later. Their bizarre and unexplained deaths are one of the most enduring true mysteries of our time. Nearly sixty years later, podcast host Nat McPherson ventures into the same mountains with her team, determined to finally solve the mystery of the Dyatlov Pass incident. Her plans are thwarted on the first night, when two trackers from her group are brutally slaughtered. The team's guide, a superstitious man from a neighboring village, blames the killings on yetis, but no one believes him. As members of Nat's team die one by one, she must figure out if there's a murderer in their midst—or something even worse—before history repeats itself and her group becomes another casualty of the infamous Dead Mountain.

Gerry Griffiths

CRYPTID ZOO

As a child, rare and unusual animals, especially cryptid creatures, always fascinated Carter Wilde. Now that he's an eccentric billionaire and runs the largest conglomerate of high-tech companies all over the world, he can finally achieve his wildest dream of building the most incredible theme park ever conceived on the planet... CRYPTID ZOO. Even though there have been apparent problems with the project, Wilde still decides to send some of his marketing employees and their families on a forced vacation to assess the theme park in preparation for Opening Day. Nick Wells and his family are some of those chosen and are about to embark on what will become the most terror-filled weekend of their lives—praying they survive. STEP RIGHT UP AND GET YOUR FREE PASS... TO CRYPTID ZOO

Check out other great

Cryptid Novels!

P.K. Hawkins

THE CRYPTID FILES

Fresh out of the academy with top marks, Agent Bradley Tennyson is expecting to have the pick of cases and investigations throughout the country. So he's shocked when instead he is assigned as the new partner to "The Crag," an agent well past his prime. He thinks the assignment is a punishment. It's anything but.Agent George Crag has been doing this job for far longer than most, and he knows what skeletons his bosses have in the closet and where the bodies are buried. He has pretty much free reign to pick his cases, and he knows exactly which one he wants to use to break in his new young partner: the disappearance and murder of a couple of college kids in a remote mountain town.Tennyson doesn't realize it, but Crag is about to introduce him to a world he never believed existed: The Cryptid Files, a world of strange monsters roaming in the night. Because these murders have been going on for a long time, and evidence is mounting that the murderer may just in fact be the legendary Bigfoot.

Gerry Griffiths

DOWN FROM BEAST MOUNTAIN

A beast with a grudge has come down from the mountain to terrorize the townsfolk of Porterville. The once sleepy town is suddenly wide awake. Sheriff Abel McGuire and game warden Grant Tanner frantically investigate one brutal slaying after another as they follow the blood trail they hope will eventually lead to the monstrous killer. But they better hurry and stop the carnage before the census taker has to come out and change the population sign on the edge of town to ZERO.

Check out other great

Cryptid Novels!

Hunter Shea

LOCH NESS REVENGE

Deep in the murky waters of Loch Ness, the creature known as Nessie has returned. Twins Natalie and Austin McQueen watched in horror as their parents were devoured by the world's most infamous lake monster. Two decades later, it's their turn to hunt the legend. But what lurks in the Loch is not what they expected. Nessie is devouring everything in and around the Loch, and it's not alone. Hell has come to the Scottish Highlands. In a fierce battle between man and monster, the world may never be the same. Praise for THEY RISE : "Outrageous, balls to the wall...made me yearn for 3D glasses and a tub of popcorn, extra butter!" – The Eyes of Madness "A fast-paced, gore-heavy splatter fest of sharksploitation." The Werd "A rocket paced horror story. I enjoyed the hell out of this book." Shotgun Logic Reviews

C.G. Mosley

BAKER COUNTY BIGFOOT CHRONICLE

Marie Bledsoe only wants her missing brother Kurt back. She'll stop at nothing to make it happen and, with the help of Kurt's friend Tony, along with Sheriff Ray Cochran, Marie embarks on a terrifying journey deep into the belly of the mysterious Walker Laboratory to find him. However, what she and her companions find lurking in the laboratory basement is beyond comprehension. There are cryptids from the forest being held captive there and something...else. Enjoy this suspenseful tale from the mind of C.G. Mosley, author of Wood Ape. Welcome back to Baker County, a place where monsters do lurk in the night!